THEFT OF THE AGE

By

GREG WALSH

THE MEPHISTO GROUP

CONTENTS

CHAPTER I.

Thwack!

Without making a sound, the pudgy, 5-O'clock shadowed
Caucasian man slumped forward like a marionette whose
puppeteer had dropped the reigns.

It was past dusk and blustery, and Sarah could count the
people she had seen on the street that night on one hand. *No
one* had seen what just happened, and she continued her walk
towards the library as casually as if she had momentarily lost
and regained her footing on a small patch of ice.

Her family lived in a quiet little village, and she had surely
walked its streets hundreds of times already in her young life.
The library where she spent countless hours on assigned and
unassigned projects and research, the few frivolities that she
allowed herself *(Gelato' in the summer, ice skating in the winter)*, and
her high school were all within her grasp on foot, and

inconspicuously. Average-looking, upper-middle-class teenage girls were about as rare in Dyersville as traffic lights or street signs, and the characters occupying the streets were all players in Sarah's big storybook of pre-engineered fiction, and treated with the same level of impersonality and detachment.

By no means a workhorse of a young woman, yet certainly never described as diminutive, Sarah's appearance would likely be described as *"ordinary"* by most- pretty, yet understated, and intentionally drab. She was not especially athletic and had not exhibited prodigy in anything specific throughout her youth.

What she lacked in flashy proficiencies, she made up for with acuity. The product of brilliant parents and the favor that moderate wealth grants to the young, Sarah had been pre-schooled, grade-schooled, and middle-schooled in the best that money could buy, and had soaked it all in… a veritable sponge, with the only idiosyncrasy being that she had either inherited or developed a questionable moral compass.

It was the kind of intelligence that could alienate a person, what she possessed; a depth of sight that might make her interesting to some, but odd, even off-putting to the majority. Nowhere in her thoughts existed trivialities such as the next school dance, who was dating who, or what song was the latest, greatest creation under the sun. Courteous, but rarely conversational, Sarah would have been lonely had she not been able to keep herself such good company. She was a student of the humanity that surrounded her, and a systems analyst of the personalities and mannerisms that defined it. She was a devout disciple of human study and a specialist in behavioral anomaly, and *those* were the tools of her trade.

The Green Tavern was the seediest bar in the upscale village, and was a daily benchmark on Sarah's walkabouts. Located at the end of the canal trail that ran from one end of the village to the other, it was a virtual certainty that she would pass it morning and night, and almost as certain that either a patron or one of the barhands would address her in some inappropriate way.

Looking back on today's incident outside the 'Tavern, she saw many areas for refinement. It was crude, and had the weather and other circumstances not been pitch perfect, it could have been quite a scene. If her imagination for retribution was going to come to life in this way, she was going to need to devote as much time and energy to the details of the projects as she did to her schoolwork, her routes between destinations, and the heirs she put on to keep her parents comforted and safely distanced from anything beyond the surface of her life.

She enjoyed doing her homework in the library. When her assigned tasks became mundane, there were years' worth of distractions... both in book and human form. Early evenings in the library were busy and bustling, with college students doing research, mothers and children reading fairy tales, and teenagers looking at the latest magazines. Even the hanging cardboard cutouts representing different pieces of famous literature and historical events were comforting and worth a thought; Mark Twain may never have guessed that Tom Sawyer would be fishing in cardboard form just a few feet from the first manned vehicle sent to the moon *(in paper Mache')*, or a knitted Jack, climbing his magic felt beanstalk.

3

The table she routinely chose was on the outermost corner of the periodicals section, with a view of the entire spread, save the 10-15 feet directly inside the main door. The learning paradox today was beginning algebra and a medical text on vital arteries and precautions to avoid their rupture during a procedure. As usual, she would fold her interesting reading inside a magazine- she chose *"Rolling Stone"*, which featured a group of forlorn-looking long haired boys on the cover. She thought briefly about dragging them by their hair behind her parents Subaru, and then her focus shifted back to the projects at hand.

Music was an important part of Sarah's life, just not *that* music. She fancied Chopin, and found endless pleasure in the explosive highs and lows that one instrument could create. She had always yearned to play music, but it was just not in her genes… a short stint at the violin in middle school had proven that of her aptitudes, musicianship was not one. When listening, she would close her eyes and imagine scaling an endless, spiraling staircase- floor by floor passing nothing but that which brought her happiness… fields of animals, both real and imaginary, frolicking in an open field, and in kind, tearing limb from limb a hapless soul that she had condemned in the recent past for any number of intolerable acts. Sarah's version of happiness had always been a dark blend of solitary, brooding enjoyment of simple pleasures, and a heavy-handed hammer of justice that had always come as naturally as eating or bathing. From the young boy she pushed into traffic after witnessing him abuse a cat at the tender age of 11 to the earlier this day event at the 'Tavern, in Sarah *existed* a right and a wrong, but she did not define *either* in a way that most would find even the remotest bit acceptable.

Occasionally, some of the more popular students would arrive in a group to the library, most likely if there was not a parent available to drive them to the mall or the local video arcade. They spoke loudly, talked of nonsense, and never re-filed any of the books they picked in the correct location. From an outsider's perspective they were Sarah's peers; from her perspective, they were as different from her as the offspring of a lesser mammal, exhibiting none of the deeper refinements that she believed to be necessary for the safe and successful navigation of life. They had no plan, and they had no goal. They had no sense of how close they could be at any moment to a fate engineered by the Gods over which no mortal had control, but that with attention and vigilance, one could possibly avert. Sarah spent each and every waking moment prepared- and preparing- for the faceless uncertainty that she was sure would be the undoing of all that strayed off the path of the righteous, or were touched by the plague of carelessness.

As the sideways glances began from the prim, garden-variety librarians, people shuffled for their coats leaving messes behind them like snail-trails. Sarah had given up long ago the idea of straightening after them- she had once actually been scolded for doing so by one of the snotty brood that ran the library. Despite her instincts she is now cautious to leave on time, unnoticed, and although it plagues her thoughts she will even occasionally leave the background to her *actual* reading out on the table. The appearance of normalcy, she had learned, is every bit as important as the act of normalcy itself... She had also learned that *"normal"* is largely defined by a series of deplorable, disorganized, and careless traits- all of which, sadly, are much more common than their mindful, attentive converse.

Bundled and ready for the journey home it had left her mind briefly that she would need walk directly by the site of her earlier incident. Approaching the scene immediately re-sharpened her wits; not ten seconds later she came up on the commotion and was redirected away from the canal trail. With not even a moment of consideration of the fact that she was full-party to the situation at hand, she quietly questioned the officer: *"Sir, I need to walk home, and if I don't take the canal path, my walk is 1.8 miles further"* she said *"May I please sneak by?"*

"I'm sorry… what is your name?" asked the officer. *"Sarah. Sarah Bidding"* *"Sarah, I am very sorry, but I am not allowed to let anyone pass inside this entrance to the trail. There was a tragedy here today, and we need to assure safety in any way possible for you folks that live in the area."* The officer seemed truly nice, and she honestly believed that he would have let her through if it would not have jeopardized his job and, he thought, her safety. *"OK then… I guess I'm in for a long walk."* She turned to go, and he shouted *"Sarah! Wait just a second dear…"* after a moment of interaction with another officer, the man she had spoken with hustled towards her and offered a ride home. Curious both to ride in the police car and attempt to pry some information out of the officer, she accepted, and they were off.

A minute or two of silence gave Sarah the opportunity to scan the entire inside of the vehicle… shotgun, mounted on dash, unlocked. Baton, retractable, stuck with Velcro to the console. Taser, charge-light illuminated green and mounted awkwardly below the radio. Two sets of handcuffs hooked on the fence which separated the front and back seats. Everything she expected to see, all with an accessibility level that surprised her. If so desired, she believed she could incapacitate this officer before he even got his hands off the wheel, as the mounting of the weapons very much favored the direction of the passenger.

"Thank you for the ride. What happened over on the path today?" she asked, meekly. *"Well Sarah, I can't tell you too much right now, but I will say that a man was killed there today, dear, and we have yet to determine much else. It is a truly peculiar situation…"* Sarah sat and listened, and when the images of the incident formed in her head, it was as if she were watching a movie, and that is about how real it seemed to her. *"…he was a well-liked guy, played sports at Dyersville High School. Sure, he'd run into some tough luck here and there, but he'd kept the job at the GT for over 3 years."*

The pause in conversation saw the officer shaking his head, and a true wave of bewilderment took his face. She offered *"I'm sorry to hear that… was it some sort of accident? I walked on that path into the village earlier today and didn't see a thing… I might have walked right by it!"* Another extended silence allowed Sarah to almost hear his thoughts, and the conflict he was going through trying to decide how much of this fearsome incident to tell such a helpless, impressionable, fragile girl. *"Dear, which house is yours?" "Oh, about 6 blocks, it's a gray two-story on the corner… with one of those old fashioned street lamps in the front…"* After a few more moments of pensive head-shaking, he decided to share. *"Sarah, dear, the man's death today was no accident- quite the contrary. I know this is as strange as snow in July around here, but the man from the bar… well, he was killed on purpose- murdered, sometime in the late afternoon. I highly doubt you would have walked by it… the first of the happy hour crew noticed him on their way in to the bar, and we were there not five minutes after we got that call. You would have for sure noticed a commotion upon walking by."* Sarah, of course, knew all these things. She knew that the happy hour traffic started at 4:45pm… she knew that the police were always just around the corner at the Main Donut shop… and she certainly knew that the death today was no accident, and also certainly not a spontaneous act of rage.

It was last summer when Sarah had been walking towards the village in a light blue dress, carrying her backpack and listening to music on her CD player. The day was delightful, and even for an off-tempered girl such as herself, was undeniably enjoyable. She allowed herself a scoop of mint chocolate Gelato' once a week in the summertime, and she was two blocks from her destination upon reaching the end of the trail. She had from ¼ mile out noticed several men gathered around the door of the tavern, but paid them little mind, as an unassuming teenager surely would not be on the radar for their obnoxiousness. No sooner had she drawn even with them than a ball- in fact, a playground ball from school- rolled across her path. She made the tactical error of looking in their direction and as soon as she did, Todd, the bar back at the tavern and ex-high-school uber-jock yelled at her… *"We were bowling for weirdo's!! We almost got one!!"*

Uproarious laughter followed, and the star treatment he received was as disgusting a spectacle as the manner in which his life would end just six months later. Sarah tipped her head down and turned away from the group, and upon doing so, was hit in the back with another ball. *"GOT ONE!!!"* she heard, followed again by coo's and heckling.

Confused and briefly upset, it wasn't until she was leaving the Gelato' stand that the kind Italian man pointed out the round stain on the back of her dress. She did not fixate on her appearance for appearance's sake, but she did present herself in a certain way to avoid drawing attention- neat, clean, well-kept and groomed... easy enough on the eyes not to be a curiosity, but as well not attractive enough to raise eyebrows.

After thanking the man kindly for making her aware, she began a mental checklist as she did with every problem in her life that she had to overcome. She knew where he worked, she knew when he worked. She knew that in the summer the bar was crowded day and night, and that during the agreeable weather there were people inside and out. She knew that any time but winter the gloves she would need to wear to execute her newly-forming plan would surely draw attention, and she also knew that any passerby would be focused more intently on their task at hand during the inclement weather. She had months to review, prepare, and decide exactly when and how good ol' Todd would pay her for the day, and the dress, that he had ruined.

II.

The end of the trail came up on the back side of the tavern, and unless one was expecting a visitor from that direction, would have no cause to face that way. The bar door swung open in the direction of the trail, and the stool that Todd sat on awaiting the arrival of the bar inhabitants would today serve as the perch for his execution.

Both from the History Channel and some intensive reading on the subject, Sarah knew that buying the tools needed for this type of project was a sure-fire way to get caught... every receipt, every clerk, every entrance into a store is a ticking time bomb. Even to purchase the rope she was to use she paid cash, purchased several other related items *(a hoist wheel, some grease, and a small how-to book on knotting)* and picked the dimmest, most uninterested looking cashier to complete the transaction.

There was an old boathouse three blocks down the canal trail from the village center and from the Green Tavern. It was used as boat storage until probably 10 years before she was born- now it was just filled with old remnants- piles of glass, lumber, a few old anchors, some railroad ties, and several odd-sized pipes used to run chain for the anchors.

She had made a pit-stop there on her walk home from the library the previous night. After surveying the contents months prior, she determined that a railroad stake taken from one of the old rotted ties and a short length of pipe *(when married with the rope she brought)* would be a swift, untraceable, and manageable tool for a 5"5, 105-pound 17-year old to wield. The stake fit almost too well in one of the chain holes in the length of pipe, and Sarah used her knotting book to assure that it was fixed and fastened every which way possible. She wore leather gloves- presumably the same ones she would be wearing tomorrow. They were intentionally several sizes too big- should all go awry and someone was to find them and miraculously link them to her, no sense could be made of the sizing discrepancy.

She stashed the crude axe-like tool underneath a pile of shingles inside the boathouse and would conceal it with her long overcoat tomorrow… the forecast was cloudy with snow showers, and for the intents and purposes of the day, was a forecast she could only have wished for. Her preparations were complete, and this night was the last one before she was to clear up a bothersome issue that had been lingering since last summer. She was nervous with anticipation, yet also calm and confident with her thoroughness and planning.

Bedtime was approaching, and she began her checklist early to assure a full night sleep and an early wake. Her earplugs were new, and she had changed the batteries in her flashlight the previous week. Her KA-BAR fixed blade military knife lay hidden in plain sight, fastened in its leather case to the wall behind her nightstand; she had procured it in a trade with one of her classmates whose father was an ex-Marine corps Sergeant. A prize of all prizes to her, she traded it even-up for several old record albums her parents had been storing in the basement. She could not fathom in her wildest dreams how someone could give up such a splendid treasure for some musty old records... especially *The Beatles*, who apparently just sang about love, peace, and happiness, disguised in metaphors and subtle jabs at the *"system"*. She could not even feign interest in such things, and often wondered about her classmates that would wear the logo of a certain band on their clothing. Did they really want to be inexplicably associated with *everything* that band had to say? Did that mean that they themselves had nothing to say at all, and were letting a group of people who in all likelihood couldn't care if they live or die, speak their piece? It just seemed thoughtless to her, and also confusing that something so superficial could influence someone enough to seek out a shirt bearing its' image.

Safely nestled in her bed and content with her preparation, she slept peacefully, and again dreamed of her never-ending spiral staircase; her nocturnal paradox of child-like fantasy and inquisition-style brutality... neatly wrapped up, at least right now, in a blue flannel comforter and Sailboat pajamas.

III.

She awoke to the unusual sight of her mother offering breakfast. Graciously accepting, since saving her the 15 minutes of fixing it herself will allow her a dry run of the afternoon's activities, she ate, dressed, interacted briefly with her parents, and made way.

The weather was as prescribed... cold and dreary, with snow looming overhead. Her parents often questioned her choice to walk to school, even in the harshest of weather, but being hardworking people, they also admired her spirit. She credited her parents greatly for instilling such values- had her influence been different, who's to say what she would have become. Her regimentation and thoroughness could have been handed down from either chromosome; however her ability to play coy, distracted, and ordinary was certainly a gift from her mother. A successful engineer, though often taken lightly based on pleasantness of appearance, her mother had a sweet, yet take no prisoners, approach to almost everything- a demeanor that had propelled her to heights in her career and no doubt had also kept her interesting to her husband for 21 years.

The walk today was longer than usual. Sarah's choice in footwear was one of conflict- sneakers would certainly behoove her in the event of a mishap or a sighting, however her boots certainly would have made the better choice as far as comfort and warmth. Sneakers it was... comfort would come later once she had achieved her goal and was safe in her room in the evening. Her feet were soaked already, the puddles flowing like winding, parallel rivers, racing towards a finish line. It was only two blocks until the sidewalk into town began, and no more time could be wasted worrying about wet feet...

As she approached the boathouse she set her stopwatch, waited 45 seconds *(presumably the time it would take her to dislodge and conceal her tool)*, and then began to walk briskly towards the door of the tavern, looking right then left until 10 feet before her destination. She paused for five seconds a few steps from the door, then ran at full gait up the walk, right on Main Street, and down the stairs that led underneath the bridge.

Two minutes, 15 seconds... 10 seconds faster than her previous dry run. The only possible variable was the potential snow, but what it may cause in delay, it added in camouflage.

Sarah arrived at school a bit early, used the time to hold her shoes up in front of the hand dryer in the ladies room, and set everything else aside for the next six hours.

IV.

2:30pm hit on the clock in what seemed like a matter of minutes. Journalism was her last class of the day. In addition to thoroughly enjoying the work she admired the teacher, Mr. Mahoney, and his dedication to putting forth truth, and allowing even the most amateur of writer their say in the paper, provided their concept was sound. It was also one of the few classes in her entire high school career where she was not an anomaly- all participants were thoughtful, studious, and even quite sipid- a mindset of questioning all things is what seemed to bring them to Mr. Mahoney's class.

CHAPTER I

Today, she would spend post-class time in the library at the high school, leave at 4:15pm, walk for 11 minutes... and then shortly after, arrive at the Public Library on Main Street. Not to be distracted, she wore headphones while reading at her table in the corner. They were attached to nothing- the cord hanging free inside her backpack; often she would wear headphones to prevent conversations with strangers, however she was wary of listening to music in public while her attention would be better spent on her surroundings.

As the schoolday itself did, her time after flew by as if on fast forward- before she knew it, she was walking down the canal trail and was only 75 yards from the boathouse. Her watch praised her diligence; she was poised to arrive at her destination at exactly 4:25pm- one minute early, and precisely when she expected to. Snow had begun to fall, and a gray, east coast fog had set. Sarah said a brief and silent thank you to whoever in the solar system graced her with such blessings. She made quick work of uncovering her tool and concealing it under her coat, took two deep breaths, and set out.

As soon as she left the boathouse she saw Todd sitting, back towards her, as expected. All the groundwork had been laid, all the pieces had been placed carefully in the puzzle... short of human interference, execution of her task would be seamless.

Walking at brisk, deliberate pace, she was quickly within indoor-voice speaking distance of her target. Readying her hands on the pipe she breathed deeply and quietly, removed the tool from her coat, sped her gait, and drove the railroad stake through the base of Todd's skull like a knife being shoved into a ripe melon.

CHAPTER II.

All persons under 21 were ordered to return to their homes before 9PM in the wake of the incident in the Village. Annoying in the sense of it being an unjustified order to be followed without question, this also interfered with the library closing time, and Sarah's walk home.

She loathed Todd, and blamed him for the silly restrictions his mishap had set in motion. Neck deep in analyzing ways around the curfew, she didn't even notice that she had been in the shower for almost 20 minutes. Panicked and hurried to the point of a misstep in the bathroom, she almost fell getting out of the shower. She scolded herself, reminding that most household accidents occur in the bathroom, and in the scheme of things it is the last place she should be trying to make up time. Luckily she had pre-planned an outfit, and the weather dictated a hat... she was dressed, had packed snacks in her backpack for the walk, and was out the door just six minutes late. Looking back on the 15 minute shower extension, the minor overall delay seemed to be just a slap on the wrist. Had it happened on a day when no outfit was planned, and she needed to fix her hair, there is a chance that she may have actually been late for school. The situation at the tavern had set into motion a chain of unmanageable events, and it was those events, and nothing more, that made Sarah regretful of what she had done.

Her plan all along was to ignore the incident as if it had never happened because, for all intents and purposes, it hadn't. Her gloves had been burned into dust, the weapon was left at the scene and of course had no fingerprints or any other definitive markings, and it was cold enough that there was no blood spatter on anything else she had worn that day. The only evidence of it ever happening was right now sprinkled in her mothers' garden like guilty, charred little snowflakes, drifting further and further into oblivion with each moment that the moisture of winter continued. She was resolute- she would ignore all this foolishness and go about her regular business. Should she be scolded for non-compliance to the new rules, she would simply flip the switch she possessed *(thanks to her mother)* and become a little sweet thing… adding enough uncomfortable sexual undertone that any man who should dare question her would feel compelled under his better judgment to abort mission and move away.

The situation did not exist, because proof of it being linked to her in any way, shape or form did not exist. Period.

II.

High school was a turbulent time. Add to the pressures of the real world the pressure of social acceptance, looking right, acting right, and carrying the right associations and you have an intense emotional trail mix, filled with the sweet and the salty and everything in between. Many of the students were of the impressionable mindset that Todd was a God; a legend of some sorts, and in some twisted and dysfunctional way, he was being made to have died a martyr. There were signs posted in the halls *"Remembering #28" (who, by the way, ended up being a 2nd string defensive lineman- Sarah had checked),* and chastising anyone who would snuff out such a bright, soaring beacon of life and worth. Good fucking God, she thought... only such a coarse curse word was emphatic enough to paint the emotion she was contending with. *Fuck.* Not something she usually allowed to creep in her head and her mental dialogue, and NEVER in her spoken word, however she was in a place and contending with a feeling that made it seem warranted, and almost irreplaceable.

Some of the fervor died down later in the week, but the curfew stood, and there was still an acute and dynamic police presence everywhere she walked and looked. There had been a profile released on the suspected killer- mid/late 20's *(just like the victim),* Caucasian, large, well-muscled build. They were touting the weapon as primitive, and portraying its wielder a beastly, hulking man. Motive? They had actually *suggested,* on *television,* that the motive may have been a *more than six-year-old high school football rivalry.* Perfect, yet at the same time, so disturbing and inept that in itself it angered Sarah beyond explanation.

Colleges locally were abuzz with talk of students being pulled out of classes and interviewed by police simply for playing on a different town's football team during the years Todd had played in Dyersville. Scores of nonsensical lawsuits followed the unwarranted interrogations. Everyone was distraught, and some were just projecting the blame further from the truth than others... The ones winning the *"Projecting the Blame"* world-title seemed to be the Dyersville police.

Looked at through any sort of reasonable, realistic eye, the football rivalry killer theory was absurd. Save one season in the '87-'88 school year when Dyersville went to states, only to lose to Cherokee by 30-some-odd points, the football program had been a less funny incarnation of the Bad News Bears- seasons with one or no wins, scuffles in the stands and even occasionally on the field- no one cared, or worried, about the Dyersville High School football team, past or present. Sarah understood the mentality- when something is too horrible to fathom, the brain sometimes starts grasping at scenarios that would, in clear and unclouded judgment, make no sense.

The only other violence-related deaths in recent town history were: 1. A betrayed spouse who hacked her husband's arm with a butcher knife after learning of his infidelity, only to have him die from complications of gang green several weeks later *(1991)*. 2. A hunting incident in which some teenage boys were playing military in the woods and one of them was mistaken for a deer by a local hunter... no charges were filed *(1999)*. 3. A fistfight in the bowling alley that led to one man tumbling to the ground and striking his head on the corner of a bench seat *(2002)*.

All were looked at as minor tragedies, but *none*- not even the knife assault- was an act of premeditated, conscious-less violence, with death being the full intention.

Trying to drum up some sort of sentiment, or even relate to the feelings now running rampant in her community, Sarah's mind wandered back to her at 11, and the boy she had pushed in front of the brown Buick station wagon down on Salt Road. The boy was 13, and they had often played in the same areas.

There was a small park at the entrance to a large wooded area on the outskirts of town, and many families would convene there on weekends to picnic, socialize, and show off their youngsters. The boy had a strange name- Antonio Mariposa. She remembered it so specifically because until she started learning Spanish in 7th grade, she had always thought it was meant to be a girls' name. Antonio would play with the younger kids, often pushing his way on to one of the three swings at the playground, and often showering unsuspecting sliders with sand and dirt as they reached the bottom of their ride. Sarah always thought he was just a mean boy, angry because he had a girls' name, but his aggression never directed itself at her so she left it alone.

Her parents had planned a picnic one Saturday in the early fall, and although she valued and adored time completely alone in the house, she joined them. Rain was in the forecast, but they proceeded unhindered, and were pleased to find the picnic area and the park virtually uninhabited. Sarah's parents fixed the meal, played a half hour of Frisbee, and then set off for a walk in the woods leaving her to play. She climbed to the highest point on the jungle gym and sat observing the traffic on the road in front of her, looking at the tracks of cookie-cutter houses and rows of tin can cars, and imagining the scores of fanciful creatures that existed beyond human sight in the vast woods.

Her thoughts were interrupted by the click-clack of playing cards taped into the spokes of Antonio's bike as he approached the park. He looked immediately disappointed that there was no one present to play with or torment. After waving at Sarah out of forced courtesy, he began scouring the area for entertainment. Sarah slipped back into her thoughts, enjoying

CHAPTER II

the unusual vantage point from the height of her perch, and
soaking in the pre-rain smell that had crept through the woods.

Several minutes later, a sharp, pained yowl shook Sarah from
her daze. She looked immediately to the road, as her first
thought was that something had been run over trying to cross.
Seeing nothing she began climbing down, and upon turning
180 degrees during her descent, she saw Antonio holding the
tail of a small brown cat and whipping it with a thin tree
branch. The cat was livid- screeching and struggling- but was
small enough that Antonio was able to keep it secure. Sarah's
eyes momentarily blurred in anger, and then began to re-focus,
almost as if her corneas had been spinning and needed time to
settle back in straight. She ran at Antonio waving her arms,
hoping to distract him enough to free the cat, but it was no
use. The cat was weakening, and there were visible lacerations
on its' head and face from the stick. Sarah changed course to
try to distract the boy *"Man! That cat is so mad! I can't believe you
can hold it while it's thrashing around like that!"* *"Oh,"* Antonio said
*"my sisters and cousins have cats, and I mess with them all the time. This
one is small."* Sarah feigned interest once more *"You don't want to
kill it, though, I think it's probably somebody's pet! Let's go ride your
bike."* *"The cat is dumb; it came over to me looking for food and didn't
even run when I whacked it the first time. It doesn't matter what happens
to it…"*

Following the statement he released the cat, who then hobbled
slowly off towards the woods. Antonio seemed interested in
having a playmate and the prospect, luckily, had overwhelmed
his desire to torture the cat. They walked together towards his
bike, which was standing with a kickstand on the gravel beside
the road. *"Wow!"* Sarah exclaimed, for the benefit of the cat
"That is a nice bike! Is it new?" *"No, it's just a stupid mountain bike I*

got from my cousin. The bike I WANTED was a BMX, but my stupid parents got me this. It's too big, and I can't jump it at all. It sucks." The severity of Sarah's feelings were surprising her. She had no interest in playing with Antonio, and at that moment, all she wanted to do was hurt him like he had hurt the cat. She stepped several feet back, as if he could hear her thoughts and would be alarmed, but she quickly noticed that he was distracted by the bike, and re-fastening the tape on one of the playing cards.

He was right... the bike WAS too big. Watching him mount it looked like he was climbing on to a Clydesdale, and each of his first few pedals looked like he might tip over and fall flat. Watching him ride, scowling, and just generally being a mean, pointless lout, she thought about sticking a branch in his spokes and then running into the woods. By the time he could get to her it is likely that her parents would have returned. She snuck off behind the entrance sign to the park and grabbed a durable branch. On Antonio's next pass, she crept alongside him and shoved the stick between his spokes, causing him to jolt and fly forward off the bike. He got up furious, but instead of giving chase, he bent down to survey damage to his bike. Mumbling the whole time, Antonio had called Sarah a *"cunt"* under his breath- this was a term she had never heard, but she could infer what it meant. His head was facing her, bent down with the bike at his feet and his back towards the road. They were both partially shielded from view by the large park entry sign and without giving it a second thought, Sarah struck Antonio in the head with the tree branch using a swift downward chop. He grunted and stumbled backwards and at that very moment, as if it had appeared out of her imagination, a car careened around an adjacent corner and plowed through him as he staggered in the road. Traveling much too fast for the rural setting, the car had no chance of stopping, and Antonio was still too dazed from the blow to the head to even see it coming. Sarah ran as fast as she could into the woods, knowing that the car did not see her and that she could avoid involvement if she wasn't within eyesight of the *"accident"*. She heard screaming, and car horns blowing, but she didn't turn. She ran as far and as fast as she could, all the while thinking about avoiding blame and trouble, and nothing about the boy that had just been run down in front of the park.

Finding a big Birch tree and sitting at the bottom as if she had just crossed a finish line, Sarah's pulse was racing, her heart was pounding, and her mind was a tornado of thoughts and feelings... fear, panic, wonderment... elation... relief... comfort... closure. Scanning quickly through the emotions that would be deemed acceptable in such a situation, she instead quickly settled and stayed on ones that expressed the feeling of liberation she was experiencing for eliminating Antonio. She thought of the kids on the school playground that would be happy not to see him during recess, she thought of the silliness of his girls name, she thought of the freedom she would feel knowing he was not going to bother her... and she thought of the cat, who had now been vindicated, regardless of whether it had lived or died after wandering in to the woods.

Several moments later she heard sirens approaching and saw her parents, hands clasped together, running towards the road. At that moment, they were imagining that their only child was dead, or injured, and Sarah was trying unsuccessfully to relate to what they might have been feeling. The sirens she heard were a mere formality... the boy had flown half a block when struck and looked like a rag doll, lying in a pile on the rough gravel of the rural, barely two-way street.

After waiting until she was sure the situation had been deemed an unfortunate accident, she walked back towards the park entrance, and her parents. They embraced and squeezed her until her insides hurt. The only remorse she felt towards the entire situation came when she realized that Antonio's parents would never again feel relief and joy at the safety of their son.

It had been months, maybe even years, since she had gone through that day in her mind, and doing so in combination with the feelings she was keeping at bay regarding the incident at the tavern had made her eyes heavy and her brain weary.

Sarah drifted to sleep turbulently, dwelling on and fully aware of the fact that she had now twice, with her own hands and of sound mind, taken a human life.

CHAPTER III.

Every expert living in the continental United States had now commented and armchair quarterbacked the incident in Dyersville. Sarah was expecting to hear next from Art Bell, and possibly even Agatha Christie regarding possible suspects, motives, and escape routes. The Dyersville Police had been made out to be veritable super-sleuths, and in kind, the killer had begun to be portrayed as a criminal mastermind- the suggestion had even been made that HE *(there was no debate over THIS…)* had left *by boat* in the winter, with no functioning dock nearby. Suffice it to say that Sarah was the furthest thing from the suspect radar…they'd have to go through an entire gender, and then start with all the female athletes, sift through the droves of women he had surely verbally abused at the tavern… Sarah was roughly 10,000,000 in to the list of potentials.

The demeanor of those living in the small town had become curiously Big Brother-like; twice in as many weeks Sarah was picked up by an older man in a golf cart while walking on the canal trail. He was a part of the Community Patrol- a citizens group similar to Neighborhood Watch, but with golf carts, and walkie-talkies. The curfew was still in effect, though it had been relaxed a bit, and Sarah now had her late route down pat. Just once had she seen someone on her cut-through trail between neighborhoods after 9pm- A boy, presumably her age, smoking a cigarette and squatting down in front of a tree as if taking a rest during a run. It startled her, and she may even have gasped aloud, simply due to the strangeness of seeing someone for the first time on a route she had been grooming for months. The only way she noticed him was the streetlight-like flashing of the lit end of the cigarette. He nodded, did not speak, and watched her until she was out of sight; an unusual distraction to be sure, and one that stayed with her until her next trip down the path. If he was there this time, she didn't see him.

The evenings this week had been an exercise in avoiding her parents. Her birthday was coming up, and in addition to the dismay and reluctance she felt in celebrating something she had absolutely no control over, she *despised* receiving presents for it and did not have any of the information her parents were looking for regarding their search for them. She knew what her *parents* wanted for her birthday- just once, they wanted to take a group of her friends to Red Lobster, they wanted to light candles on a cake and laugh as people clapped when they magically re-lit, they wanted to look around and marvel at the stellar taste their daughter had in companions, and they wanted her to smile and tear up after receiving the gift of a lifetime. Sarah felt in some small way that she was depriving them of the enjoyment of *her* birthday, since it was a much bigger deal for them than she, but she just could not bring herself to participate. She categorically wrote the wrong day when asked the question on a survey, test, or form, and truth be told, until her mother reminded her last Wednesday over breakfast she had forgotten it was so quickly approaching.

She had not caught the driving bug yet. She enjoyed walking, and noticed that the students in her class that drove cars to school *always* had a full load… it seemed that a rite of passage was to pick up anyone that lived near you, friend or not, and that was certainly not a tradition that Sarah wanted any part of. The sole aspect of driving that enticed Sarah was the unfettered access it would create to the mall… shopping be damned- where else can you gain access to hundreds, even thousands, of people in one day and while remaining totally anonymous? The mall was a place that she felt truly comfortable and also, strangely, truly alone. It brought out the worst in people- someone could be laying in a pool of blood at the feet of a shopper, and if The Gap was having a sale, the blood would continue to pour. 10-year-old girls were dressed like the prostitutes she had seen in the movies, and the people that worked there acted as if they were participating in some sort of humanitarian effort or special government project… too good to even look at you unless you too were wearing a name on your shirt in raised letters on a little plastic plate.

Those things endeared the mall to her. She could not, even if she tried, be strange or off-putting in comparison. She would have to run screaming and on fire from end to end in order for people to even notice her presence… and that was perfect. She was content to live vicariously through their groups of friends, and socialize by osmosis.

From even a safe distance, Sarah prided herself on being able to be a fly on the wall of a conversation. Reading the language and mannerisms she could know with certainty if someone was having relationship problems, was skipping detention or some other unpleasant after school activity, or truly just there to buy jeans and a shirt for upcoming school pictures. On the rare occasion when a group would notice her watching them, she would simply smile politely and walk off, or go back to the teen magazine she always had open in her hands to act as a diversion in precisely those types of situations. When she *was* caught in the act she had often thought that the group must be flattered in a way, and likely looked at Sarah's attention as jealousy, or longing to belong to the little social circus they were all players in. She would look back over with a little more subtlety and would usually see a primped, straighter-standing group; now that they were under observation by one of the runts of the social litter, they simply *must* look and behave their best.

The rigmarole assured Sarah that she wanted nothing to do with the groups she looked at, and even less to do with the selfishness and absurd trifles that they concerned themselves with for hours on end. She knew that feeling that way made her somewhat unusual, but her thoughts always reverted back to questioning: how could *she* be unusual when *they* were so silly and flighty? The contrast was something that was on her mind often, and through it all, she *did* yearn for someone to talk to about it… someone like her, someone who *understood*.

Playmates had come and gone in her younger years though she had not had a real friend so far in her young adult life. She was casual acquaintances with several of the people that worked on the school paper, and was friendly with the older man that ran the Gelato' stand, but no one made her phone ring, no one occupied her time on the weekends, and no one walked the halls huddled up near her telling secrets or reflecting on classroom happenings. She lived, very similarly as she did with strangers in the mall, through fantasy and through fiction. Orwell's *"1984"* read as a great love story in her mind, and she often envisioned herself in the role of Julia- living a secret life, remaining anonymous, only to seek the affections of one person who understood her above all others. She had read every single piece of work that Laura Ingalls Wilder had ever penned, and was envious of each tale of a simpler time, when people behaved with courtesy and honor and treated people how they wanted to be treated themselves. The people she described were simple, yet learned, and existed for more than just the indulgence of their every want and need. *Those* were the people Sarah longed to meet but did not know how, or where. Maybe they were all around her, and she was the one that was walking off the path of righteousness. Her internal dialogue was never ending, and each step she took raised another question for which she had no answer.

II.

Journalism class was a beacon of color in Sarah's otherwise neutral days. The fascination she found in writing stories from the perspective of what she thought her peers would say and want to read was like an applied sociology experiment. She thrived in the environment, and was able to transform her bizarre and profound feelings into innocuous yet satisfying stories for the paper, week after week. She would pretend to be someone else- she would project herself into one of her fictional idols or into a student from her class, and write how she felt *they* would write; how she felt *they* would feel. Complemented often on the pieces she submitted, it was only her stark and definitive aversion to working in a group that kept her from being on-staff at the paper. Several of the editorial positions were filled with students she knew to be her intellectual inferiors, but were the bubbly and precocious sort that the position suited.

Andrew Mahoney *(same last name but no relation to the teacher)* was an editor, and also a buffoon. Routinely making spelling errors that the other editors would catch and admonish him for, he smiled his million dollar smile, mussed his politicians haircut, and all seemed to be forgotten. A swimmer and a debate team member, Andrew would push every issue for more pages relating to each; as if sports in high school needed more attention, as if they would be forgotten without him there to champion the cause. Although she enjoyed Journalism, he was the sort of bottom-feeder that Sarah assumed would be involved should she choose to pursue it in college or beyond, and she could not stand the thought of someone like that being her boss. Even though he was an editor on the paper, it was made clear in every class that Mr. Mahoney was the only *"boss"*, and that all the students were equal, regardless of title. She would watch Andrew frequently, in class and out, and she was fairly sure he thought she had a crush on him- he would often smile at her with the look of *"…I know you want me, but it could just never happen between us."* If only he knew her real feelings, if only *he* knew what *she* knew about the fragility of human life, and of the human ego under pressure. Sarah had strategized a half a dozen ways to de-smug Andrew, but she knew after all that he was merely doing what he thought he was *supposed* to do. Surely his dad, and his dad before him were equally smug poster boys that had passed their charms and traits, unintentionally and unknowingly creating an automaton whose life's path was set before him before he could even walk on his own.

CHAPTER III

Waking with a start from her daydream in the middle of the mall, she found herself staring into the pages of *Seventeen magazine* and focused on anything *but* the content. The noise that had pulled her back to earth was that of a scuffle. She turned and looked, and saw three older boys pushing and cursing at one smaller boy who was wearing a beanie cap, and carrying a huge backpack. Sarah couldn't yet figure the cause of the confrontation, but there was no mistaking the fear that ran over the lone boy's face. He had put his backpack down, almost as if he knew what came next, and didn't want any additional baggage when it happened. One of the larger boys slapped his face, and as soon as the blow was struck he covered up and started to hunch over. Sarah wanted to run over and help, attack the bullies, and run to safety with the young boy. To do so would be suicide, and would also draw a level of attention to her that she could not risk.

To watch him be tormented pained her, and she concentrated hard on the attackers so she could remember and identify them later. What happened next made Sarah blink twice and even shake her head to assure that it was real. A boy in black jeans and a black hooded sweatshirt had run through and hit the largest of the group in the head with what appeared to be a small club affixed to the end of a strap. The boy hit the ground like a dropped puppet, and the commotion gave the otherwise sitting duck time to gather his bag and flee. The new attacker was long gone by the time the struck boy made his way back to his feet, but the group ran after him nonetheless. Watching the biggest of the group try to run on wobbly legs with his arms outstretched to his sides was the most amusing thing Sarah had seen in quite some time, and she had immediate and warm feelings towards the interloper that had turned the tide on the unfair situation.

She had been meditative on the entire bus ride home from the mall. Her mind was racing, and filled with questions. Who was the boy that had attacked the attackers? How did he know what was happening? Was he watching the situation, including Sarah, from afar? If so... *how* did she miss *him*?

The bus let her off three blocks from home and she was acutely aware of her surroundings in a completely new way. She had decided that the boy being there was no mistake or coincidence, and that if he were perceptive enough to intervene at precisely the right moment, he had certainly been aware and conscious of her presence. As reality washed over during the walk, she scolded herself for being arrogant enough to think he was following or aware of her in anything more than random context. For that to be the case would mean that he was *like* her- a watcher- and that she had likely crossed unknowing paths with him before. A strange cold chill came over her, followed by a wave of fear. She ran the last block home, and burst through the door as if to narrowly escape capture.

Uncustomarily glad to see her parents sitting at the dinner table, she actually answered the questions they asked. *"How was your day, dear?"* asked her mother, ordinarily. *"Oh, pretty run of the mill, but I saw a fight at the mall and it was truly unusual. Someone ran through and hit one of the bullies as he was beating up on a small boy!"* Her parents looked as if a deaf mute child had spoken aloud for the first time. Stunned, yet eager to see if the conversation would continue, Sarah's mother probed *"Well, that certainly sounds unusual... are you hanging around people that are fighting?"* *"Oh no... no. I was reading a magazine and it just sort of erupted near me. I must have been daydreaming a bit. I didn't see how it all began."* The last two minutes were the most conversation that Sarah had allowed her parents in months, maybe longer. As they both sat, semi-stupefied at the outpouring of information, she volunteered one last nugget of unpredictability *"I've been thinking"* she declared plainly *"And I think I'd like to get my driver's license."*

CHAPTER IV.

The next weeks of Sarah's life were an exercise in scrutiny and self-evaluation. Every route she was accustomed to, every seat or nook that she spent time in, and every location that she visited was viewed with new eyes and an acutely increased sensitivity. The incident at the mall had not moved far from the front of her mind and she was certain, if she looked hard enough, that the interloper was not far from her vigilant watch. Tuesday afternoon Sarah had seen a boy fitting the description of the one she sought, and her belly rolled and twisted as she made her approach.

As she moved close a sickly, heavy smell reached her, and when the boy heard her approaching she realized that the hood he wore was only to conceal the marijuana cigarette he was smoking. She glared at him unintentionally and he scurried off, looking both confused as to why Sarah was approaching him silently and alone, and relieved that there was no repercussions for his public drug use. Disappointed but undeterred Sarah went on to the library, reassigning her seat to the back corner amongst the encyclopedias where she had an unhindered view of the entire floor plan, front door and all. The downside is that no one sat back by the encyclopedias, so there were no conversations to distract her mind from its path. The only oddity of the entire afternoon was Andrew Mahoney, dimwit Journalism student, perusing the archived magazines in a very non-casual way. Strange that he would even be *at* the library; the urgency with which he was pawing through periodical after periodical made it twice as unusual. Knowing that the school paper was on deadline that week, and that her own writing was to be turned in on Monday, her vivid imagination closed in on the common sense that he was looking for articles to submit as his own. *Brilliant*, she thought, *the idiot was going to hang himself without her even having to plant the seed.*

Sarah was very familiar with the archives in the small library. Watching patiently as Andrew narrowed the field to two or three magazines and then made his way to the copier, she made note of the specific drawers and titles he had chosen, leaving only a dozen or so titles to sift through once he returned the borrowed. A line at the copier gave her a little time to familiarize herself with the magazines contained in the drawers, and she thought it would be quite easy to identify the ones he would replace. Possibly a bit too caught up in her research, she had failed to notice Andrew coming back towards her. As her head turned he saw her without question, and veered down a different path away from the archives. She had slipped up, and was immediately angry with herself; though beyond unlikely that he would ever think that she knew his plagiaristic plan, it was still unacceptable.

She collected her things while subtly watching Andrew over her shoulder. He now sat in the new periodicals, reading a

Sports Illustrated and glancing toward the archives over its top edge. Her research would have to be continued another day. The pieces of his witless deception would be no harder to put together then- even easier perhaps once she found out his assignments for the upcoming issue of the paper.

Frustrated by her carelessness, the walk home seemed unusually long and tedious. Her mind shifted frantically from the boy she sought, to the possibility that Andrew knew what she was doing in the archives, to- surprisingly- getting her driver's license. Her journeys had new meaning now, and time spent wandering could be spent more productively motorized, and looking for her target. She knew without question that her parents would fashion her with a safe, reliable car, and she also knew that she would enjoy the private time in it and would utilize the tool to its potential. She could easily cover her entire walking route seven or eight times by car in the time it would take her on foot, and at a significantly enhanced vantage point. If the boy *did* know her routes, she would certainly have a better chance of seeing him again if he didn't know she was coming...

She arrived home just as her parents were going to bed. She said a pleasant goodnight, and retreated to her safe haven, with mind racing and wits at their end. Rest would be welcomed tonight, and she looked at it as an eraser for a day she would rather forget.

II.

Two days off could not have come at a better time. Still unreasonably fixated on her error in the library, the weekend would give things time to cool off, even if they were askew only in her mind. She would also have unfettered access to the library as no one in her class would likely be caught dead there on a weekend.

The morning had Sarah imagining a day filled with goings-on. Phone calls, socializing- all of it seemed so foreign that even when creating the scenes in her mind they seemed as improbably as riding to school on a unicorn, or finding a secret tunnel to an underground village. It was regular for Sarah to think of herself as invisible, and she was *sure* that if she concentrated on it hard enough, that she could be. Sometimes she would stand still for hours, just watching the world go by, and not be met with so much as a glance; no eye contact, no casual chatter. She *was* invisible, even if only figuratively so, and most days it suited her quite nicely. As the weekend passed, however, a sense of loneliness began washing over her… and as it set in, she began placing blame anywhere it seemed to stick. It wasn't *she* that was unusual, it was *them*… it wasn't *her* thoughts that were odd; it wasn't *her* feelings that were beyond common grasp… it was… them. She would near tears with everything she set eyes on in her room, all of it seeming to cast judgment or point out failure. All the music she had, all the books she had read- they all painted her as the anomaly. Usually it was a role that she relished, and even yearned for. To be alone was to truly be free… but free from what? She felt trapped in her mind, and a virtual prisoner in her own room, in her own house.

She had not one place to go on this earth where anyone was awaiting her arrival, not one place where she could go and just *be*. Pain was becoming profound and blinding, and she pulled the hood of her sweatshirt tight around her head in a vain effort to quiet the chaos going on inside it. Sarah closed her eyes. Today there was no endless staircase, no moral idealism. Today it was a sea of fire, burning everything that everyone loved... the people she went to school with, their parents, the boys at the mall- she wanted them to feel *nothingness*. She wanted them to sleep and wake in abandon, everything they've ever cherished burned to the ground, everyone they've ever cared for aflame in a lake of unquenchable fire and death. As she retraced the steps that had brought her to this point, Andrew crossed her mind. Too caught up in his asinine deceptions, she had let herself stray from a proven course- proven both to keep her safe, and to keep her sane. Deviating from it had led her here... and Andrew had been the cause. If he were asleep on her bed right now, she would slit his throat; she would shish kabob his heart. And she would make him ugly- as ugly as he is dumb, and as hideous to look at as it is to watch him live his trite, selfish life.

Warmth washed over her at the thought of killing Andrew, and she knew then that she must pull herself together and begin planning. Composure is paramount when planning the way she planned. Emotion displayed as it was today is unacceptable, it is frail, and it is *human*. She may be human in many ways, as her unavoidable depression today had proven, but she must abandon as many of those characteristics as she is able, both for self-preservation and to reach her goals... however ill-tempered they may be.

There is no use crying over spilled milk, she often told herself. She will always be alone, she will always be deviant. Righting the wrongs that cross her path is her role in society. Of that she was certain. Happiness, contentment... these things were myths of the uninformed, and luxuries of the ignorant. Even if they do temporarily exist Sarah knew that, ultimately, sadness would always prevail.

III.

Her shower lasted almost an hour, the last drops of hot water trickling down her back and giving way to cold; a literal and metaphorical awakening. Dressed and out the door in her usual gait, she headed to the library to complete her unfinished task. She would have only about 45 minutes before closing time, but both for safety and sanity it was important that she complete this weekend what she had unsuccessfully started last week.

She was almost positive she had noticed someone in the shadows along the path on her walk to the village, but in her current state of semi-agitation, she chalked it up to nerves.

The library was a ghost town- Sunday at 5:15pm being when most are spending time with family, or at least a TV family. Moving directly to the archives, she pulled from her bag the paper containing notes from Friday. The drawer that Andrew was digging through contained the last 12 months of *Sailing*, *Seventeen*, and *Sports Illustrated*. Taking one minute of pleasure in thinking of Andrew reading or referencing *Seventeen*, she started looking for misplaced issues of the other two titles. All she had to do was narrow down to one or two issues and wait until the paper came out next Thursday. After reading Andrew's stories, she would return and cross-reference them with the issues she had hidden. Maybe a bit too thorough, but should he connect the dots on her visit to the archives he would likely remove the evidence. She narrowed by gut feeling and haphazard misplacement three issues of *Sports Illustrated* and one issue of *Sailing* and moved them to the back of the "*Q*" archive drawer. Five minutes to spare...

Exhausted both physically and mentally, Sarah laid down on her bed to read and ended up falling asleep with the book as a pillow, and fully clothed. Nonetheless, it was one of the most restful nights in her recent memory, and she was grateful for it. She had a lot of work to do and had to be sharp; weary eyes or a weary mind would just not do.

As the week began she could not help but think of the boy. Did he go to school in Dyersville? Had he graduated? Sarah contemplated... possibly private school? He did not look old enough to be finished, but he did not look ordinary enough to be a student at her school.

School was school, each day seeming as if it could fill out the same punch card as the previous. Journalism deadline was the day's only notable event. She submitted her stories with little fanfare, and managed to not speak through the entire class save her hello and goodbye to Mr. Mahoney. Three days remained until she would maim her prey, the time until he was finished off still unknown. Surely the discovery of his potential plagiarism would be a crushing blow to the otherwise upright citizen, and he would undoubtedly be looking for the culprit; he would just as surely eventually land on Sarah.

Just as her mind had been yearning for a distraction from mundanity, a truly bizarre one was placed in front of her. A local miscreant was arrested and charged with the Green Tavern murder earlier that winter. In the 45 seconds of detail she got from the evening news her parents were watching, she learned that he had confessed, did not have an alibi, owned a rifle and several handguns, and had been in a scuffle with Todd during their tenure together in high school. The news brewed a tornado of mixed feelings in Sarah. She was hoping for a thorough, exhaustive investigation that due to the immaculate planning of the crime, yielded no results. She was hoping that if anyone *were* charged that it was a drunken playmate of Todd's, jealous over a girl or some other trivial emotional matter. Never did she hope or expect some troubled soul to fess up to it, seemingly just to escape or restitute for other turmoil or previous bad acts in his life. For that she felt sorrow; the perfection of her crime wasted, along with the life of someone probably far more interesting than the scores of idiots that remained walking the streets.

For the second night in less than a week sleep came hard and did not provide the rest and reset she sought. Had she gotten in over her head in too many unsettling situations? Was her brain simply full, and like the computer her father was always swearing at, would not work properly again until it was cleaned out? Finality, she decided, was the only way to purge the gobbelty-gook that made her brain so heavy. She must reckon the situations she had in her mind's *"open"* file so that they no longer troubled her. Easier said than done, but she had never been one to shy away from a seemingly insurmountable challenge.

CHAPTER V.

The moment of reckoning was close now. The school paper was placed on every desk and strewn on every table on Thursday morning before even the very first student crossed the threshold. In mere hours the seeds of deceit that Andrew had sown would be rearing their heads, unstoppable, with thousands of witnesses to their being. The seconds ticked slowly and thunderously in Sarah's mind, the passing of each marking a moment closer to her after school sprint to the library. Complimented by several strangers on her inclusions in this month's paper, she wandered the halls startled by the unfamiliarity of random praise, and also of the recognition of her as *"her"*. She had always thought that her name being in the paper was purely incidental, and didn't actually personalize anything. People she did not know did in fact know her- this discovery made her uneasy, although there was a brief moment when she felt grateful for their kind words.

Mahoney's class was one of examination today- they collectively reviewed their work, picked out faults- typos, print errors, sequential problems caused by a missing page number, etc.

Overall, they had fared extremely well. Two typos and one numerical error in separating a multi-page story and that was it-near perfection compared to several issues last year where there were misspellings on every page and in fact several story endings that did not make it in at all. The class let out on a positive note, with compliments all around, and a sense of solidarity and relief that visited only occasionally in a high school setting.

The previous hour was put aside as soon as the bell rang. Without being overt, it was off to the races. Coat in tow, and backpack lightened by the absence of homework completed throughout the day during other classes, Sarah was out the side door and on the path to the library by 2:38pm. She arrived to some sort of after-school reading club for what looked to be 7th and 8th graders. The story today was *"Superfudge"*; a great book, but likely one that each of them had read a dozen or so times by that age. There was a bustling amongst the students and attention focused anywhere but the stately middle-aged woman reading aloud. Sarah reached the archives at 2:57pm and found several groups of the inattentive junior high students seated together on the floor in the secluded aisle. She did not look towards them, and acted as casual and unassuming as she possibly could after walking as fast as her legs would carry her for close to 18 minutes.

As she expected, her hidden volumes had not been re-filed. The logistics of simultaneously reading the school paper and scanning the magazines' indexes for similarities proved an unexpected challenge, but with some quick fold work, she isolated the first several paragraphs of Andrew's three articles. One in particular- a quite involved narrative on baseball rules and how they had changed from the early 1900's to present-day- seemed much too wordy and learned to be Andrew's, with the exception of the opening paragraph. She put down *Sailing* and focused on *Sports Illustrated*. Sure enough, the article was found in one of the misplaced issues- opening sentences were changed, but past that, a mirror image. Even the statistics were copied and submitted word-for-word. Her ears got hot as she confirmed her suspicions of piracy... she held in her hand an 8-½ x 11 order of execution for Andrew Mahoney, and her only further consideration was how to present it convincingly.

She did not want Mr. Mahoney to think her a snoop or a busybody, but she was sure that he would want information like this brought to light. She developed a plan that started with the theft of the back-issue from the library and whose next step was one of nearly-common sense: Of course with a contributing daughter, her father read the paper. Being an avid sports fan, he mentioned the similarity of an article in the sports section to something he had read in a magazine. Not able to get it out of his mind, he eventually located the issue, and lo-and-behold... a perfect match. It was Sarah's *duty* to inform her teacher and mentor, if not only for the integrity of their work, but for the potential legal pitfalls that the school may endure upon the incidents discovery. Or so she told herself.

Sarah collected her things and made her way home, filled with a sense of relief that there had not been any further trip-ups in securing the damning information. The temperature was slightly warmer; a possible sign of spring on its way, and the walk was pleasant. She took her hood down and although it would likely be hood weather for another month, the crisp air was refreshing and gave her energy. Coming up on the darkest and most isolated part of her walk, she switched on, making sure that she was alone and aware of her surroundings. She had only walked one block down the trail when she spotted the intermittent glow of a cigarette burning across the canal in a small wooded area. Just past dusk, she was able to make out a motionless figure but nothing more, the cigarette being the only real clue that anyone was there at all. She stopped in her tracks and stared, knowing with a puzzling certainty that it was the boy- the very same she had seen in the woods smoking before, the very same that she felt may have changed the course of events during the incident at the mall. He did not move as she stared, and although darkness and distance separated them, she felt more in touch with the vague smoking shadow than she had felt with anyone. Her ears went from cool to warm; she was almost sure they were glowing red in the dark, just like the lit end of his smoke. She wanted to yell, she wanted to risk the climb down the small rocky bluff and test the ice as she crossed the canal, but neither would happen. Just a stare, reciprocated and lengthy, and a new distraction as Sarah's mind wandered to the next potential meeting before she was five feet from the last. After standing and staring for nearly a half hour, she walked on, and the boy stayed.

Almost bursting with desire to speak with someone after her silent contact, Sarah ran immediately to her dad as she entered the house. *"Dad, do you read 'Sports Illustrated'?"* Looking positively baffled first that Sarah was talking to him, and second that she had expressed any interest in his life, he answered *"Well, I know it probably strikes you as strange, but yes... I am positively the least athletic person I know, but having a subscription to SI is almost a male duty."* Relieved, and leaving her father in dismay, she barked a quick thank you and retreated to her room. Today had been quite a day, and tomorrow had promise also. Her resolution to close the open doors seemed to be going as planned, and had certainly left her in a much more placid mental state. Still lingering was the feeling of excitement and discovery from her chance meeting along the canal, and although she read nearly 75 pages of her book, her mind was anywhere BUT the plight of the youngsters in Stephen King's *"It"*. She lay awake for hours, staring at the glow-in- the-dark stars on her bedroom ceiling and wondering everything there was to wonder about *"her"* boy. As she drifted off to sleep she pictured the two of them driving in a car, music blaring, with no set destination and not a single care in either of their minds.

II.

Sarah awoke purposefully, her mind immediately fixed on the method and timing of today's disclosure to Mr. Mahoney. She readied quickly, skipping breakfast and opting for a snack en route to school, her hope being to meet the teacher before the first bell rang; she wanted to leave no chance of her nefarious finding remaining hidden for another day. Arriving at school 23 minutes before start of day and entering through the un-monitored side doors, her only challenge was locating Mahoney with enough time before 1st period to spell out her story. Knowing him as one that prepared for class in the classroom and not in the teachers' lounge, she tried there first, and with success. The door was locked, but Mr. Mahoney was in, and alone.

He looked startled to see Sarah's face peeking at him through the small rectangular window, and immediately scurried over to let her in. Still looking concerned, he was quick to ask if she was alright, and if there was anyone after her. She found his train of thought strange, much as hers might have been in a similar situation, and she quickly assured him of her well-being. Her safety confirmed, Mahoney asked her what WAS wrong, since students were not allowed in the building at this time without a scheduled teacher meeting. She looked at her shoes and shrugged uncomfortably, as she thought a student questioning their actions might do, and then she spoke.

"Mr. Mahoney, something came up over the weekend, and I had to come in early to talk to you about it. My father read our paper over the weekend, and on Sunday he sat me down and asked if I knew Andrew Mahoney." She stammered, intentionally, and continued her tale. *"He was reading Andrew's baseball story and said it rang a bell to him. By the time I had sat down with him, he had found an issue of 'Sports Illustrated'... the issue he handed me had the same article as Andrew's, and it was from 2006."* She had completed phase one successfully. She had spoken as if conflicted, looked as if pained, and stopped as if she was reluctant to say more. *"Sarah, you DO realize what you've just told me here? That is a VERY serious thing you've said, and you certainly seem like you might be questioning your decision to say it."* Sarah again looked at the ground, silently grateful that his response was almost word-for-word what she expected. *"I didn't even know how to begin... so... I tore the pages out of the magazine and brought them to you. I was just so surprised by the whole thing, I didn't know if I should just ignore it... it came to me yesterday evening that you, or even the other editors, could possibly get in some sort of trouble should anyone ever find out. That is when I decided to tell you."* As she handed the torn pages to Mr. Mahoney she manufactured a sad, guilt-ridden look on her face to seem as if she felt great remorse at turning in one of her fellow journalists. Mr. Mahoney returned in kind with a sympathetic and slightly sad look of approval, nodding his head and taking

the pages from Sarah's hands. He looked as if he had found reprieve as he was reading the non-matching first paragraphs, but as he continued his brow furrowed, and he stared intently at the pages, almost looking as if he were hoping they would tell him what to do next.

"Sarah, I am certainly not happy about this discovery… but thank you for bringing it to my attention. It will of course be kept privately between you and I, and I appreciate your concern for me and your fellow classmates. This is INDEED a very serious issue, and I need to ask you not to speak about it to anyone, and trust that it will be handled immediately." Sarah nodded sullenly and left quickly, with exactly four minutes to make it to 1st period. Confident about her handling of the situation she felt the relief of another door closed. Even though it would likely be several periods before Andrew's inquisition, the trap was irrevocably set. Sarah pondered playfully the idea of Andrew's smug demeanor being squashed, and the stammering idiot he would likely become when trying to justify his sloppy indiscretions. He would likely never be the same, and that is *exactly* what Sarah wanted.

She would wait patiently for 8th period Journalism class. The time leading up to it would be tedious; she had to seem at ease, at least as much so as usual, and also would need to express the same abject horror and surprise as the rest of the class when told of the reason behind Andrew's likely absence. All eyes would likely be on Mr. Mahoney and then would just as likely erupt into conversation. She just needed to not seem odd during the turmoil… and certainly not happy, grateful, or fulfilled; those feelings would need to wait to be indulged at home.

III.

The first scuttlebutt Sarah heard regarding the incident was during lunch. She was a part of the third lunch period, which was the 7th period of the day. She enjoyed the late lunch- it gave her time to roam and explore after 8th period with no worry of getting hungry again until she found her way home. As she assumed happened in lunchrooms everywhere, people were creatures of habit and sat in the same seats, day after day. Sarah sat back to the wall on the non-jukebox side of the cafeteria. Several of the girls from her journalism class sat kitty-corner from her, and she could easily overhear their conversations as long as nothing too obnoxious was playing. It was easy listening today, and that made eavesdropping simple. One of the girls had heard that someone in Journalism 8 *(that is what their class was called)* got caught plagiarizing a story. She didn't know who, but did know that they had already been suspended, and switched from Journalism to study hall for the rest of the year. The group exchanged horrified commentary about the situation, and immediately started throwing out their takes on the identity of the guilty party. One of the girls, Meghan *(with an "H", she was always quick to point out...)* chimed *"It was probably Timothy. He's weird, and he acts SO smart, but his stories are always just about bands and stuff. He probably copied some reviews from 'Rolling Stone' or something."* Timothy was the only person in her class that she had ever spoken to willfully- he was a small, messy-haired boy that would obviously have rather been writing fiction or poetry, but writing music reviews for the school paper was better than nothing. He was nice, quiet, and a talented writer. It made sense that the girls singled him out immediately, and that Andrew did not even come up as an option. The now blaring music drowned out any further access to their idle chatter, but all Sarah needed was to hear that the information is under foot. The truth would make its way to center stage by the end of the day.

A disclosure of such magnitude and on such a public scale had given Sarah very uncustomary feelings of insecurity. Walking the halls between 7th and 8th periods, she felt as if there were eyes on her... as if she had been outed as the snitch in the same turn as Andrew had been fingered as the plagiarist. She hunched her head, but did not dare put her hood on, as she felt it may draw attention and raise suspicions. Why was she hiding, they would wonder? Sure, she was a private and very solitary person, but she had very seldom been the kind that would hide behind dark clothing, mops of hair, or hoods. The kind that DID isolate themselves in that manner, she had often observed, actually did so TO be noticed and not the other way around. They wanted to be talked to and accepted so badly that they were willing to modify appearances to an overt degree. Sarah disliked the very idea- she felt it emotionally dishonest; a *"boy who cried wolf"* scenario, and also thoroughly transparent.

If she wanted to be alone, she would let people know *without* telling them... she would simply *be* alone- not welcoming or baiting conversation, not making eye contact, and not doing anything that would evoke response or interest from those around her. It was a social art in and of itself; similar to the art of small talk, or the rigors of being a gifted conversationalist. If she chose to talk she could of course do so with poise and dexterity, but on most occasions she chose not to and took pride in the skill needed to execute that choice.

The time had come- she found herself on auto-pilot and just several yards from Journalism 8.

7th period lunch, and anything discussed within, were already absent from her mind and she briefly questioned how she had managed to get through the day so far detached from her mental faculties. She was consumed with the outing of Andrew Mahoney, and it was now just moments away. Her back was hot, she felt the slightest bit of perspiration on the lower part of it, and also on her stomach. Nothing she had ever done had brought her nerves to this height... not the incident at the 'Tavern, not the sight of her boy in the woods across the canal, and not even the moment of worry when Andrew had sighted her at the archives. This was new. She felt *alive*; her generally cool temperature had risen, and she felt an anxiousness that tingled in even the most private regions of her body. Maintaining composure and calmness until the announcement was made would be a tall task. Sarah had begun breathing rhythmically in order to lower her pulse, and had taken her backpack off in an effort to lower the temperature on her back. She sat, notebook out and pen in hand waiting for the arrival of the executioner. Sure, she had set the series of events in motion, but the man in the black hood that wielded the axe was Mr. Mahoney. Five minutes late and looking flustered, in he came.

IV.

With a dignified and stern look on his face, Mr. Mahoney stood in front of the silent class with a copy of last week's paper in his hands. The tone of the room was bleak, and that meant *(or at least Sarah took it to mean)* some of the class was already aware of the situation at hand. After several moments of staring at the paper, Mr. Mahoney spoke. *"I have been a Journalism teacher and advisor on the paper here in Dyersville for 13 years, and not once, until today, has the integrity of our paper's content been called into question."* He said with conviction. *"There have been quotes printed unintentionally without bibliographies several times, a few pictures run before final permission was granted, but nothing, NOTHING like what has occurred today."*

His tone had changed from remorse to frustration, and his next few sentences had a sharp bite. *"Your classmate, Andrew Mahoney, has intentionally put our paper and reputations in jeopardy by plagiarizing a story in last week's paper directly from the pages of a 2006 issue of* Sports Illustrated. *He even went so far as to change the opening paragraph to avoid detection, but thankfully it was discovered internally so we can make the necessary apologies with no further consequences to the paper or the school."* Seemingly relieved to have gotten it out, the kind, helpful demeanor returned *"Guys, as you know, Journalism is not a required course. You chose to be here. You decided that amongst all the other classes offered to fill this requirement that Journalism was something you wanted to commit your time and energy to this year. I am grateful that you made that decision, and it is truly a pleasure to work with all of you, however I must say this- should you EVER feel that stealing even so much as a sentence from another writers work is a suitable solution to avoid missing deadline or not completing a story, you need to get up and walk out this door RIGHT NOW!"* The anger had resurfaced and it must have been as uncustomary for him to put forth as it was for the class to experience, because his face was red, and everyone's mouths were agape. *"Does everyone understand the importance of what I have just said?"* Nods abounded, and not one person chose to exit.

"Andrew has been suspended for one week, and will not be returning to Journalism 8. There will be no legal repercussions for what he did, but as I mentioned, that is purely by the good fortune that we discovered and handled the situation internally. Had the discovery been made on a larger scale…" (This was actually possible, because the Dyersville paper was ranked one of the top 10 student papers in the nation, and therefore was sent each month for review by a

national board) *"…we could have been fined, and at the very least lost our footing in the national rankings."* The class of non-trouble makers, '*A*' students, and upright citizens were scared straight, and as Sarah looked around, everyone was ghost white and looked a little sick. Mr. Mahoney ended the day's class with a final statement. *"This is the last we are going to talk about this, but I do not want it to be the last you think about it. This is a lesson you should take with you as long as your career in writing of any kind lasts. I am grateful to the person that made this discovery, as uncomfortable as it is, because it will now assure that none of you will ever make this mistake yourselves. Back on track tomorrow, next deadline is 20 days out."* 15 minutes before the final bell of the day the class had ended, and the mood was a combination of shock and disbelief. Students were required to stay in their 8th period rooms until the bell rang, and there was not a word said, nor did a student stir until it did. Just a few hours ago Andrew Mahoney had been a *member* of the upright citizens of Journalism 8… now, in addition to the punishment itself, there were 20 firsthand accounts of his fall from grace. By this time tomorrow the entire school would know of the wrongdoing, and by the time Andrew returned from suspension, he would be looked at through entirely different eyes by the students of Dyersville High School.

CHAPTER VI.

Tuesday felt like it should be Friday after all the anxiety and eventfulness of the previous day. Relieved that it had gone as planned, and intrigued by the new feelings the culmination of the situation had brought on, Sarah was feeling different today and it must have come across. Several boys had said hello to her unexpectedly throughout the morning, and after she had ruled out the idea that they were playing a joke, she was left questioning their true motives. In addition, she had already heard several groups talking about Andrew as she passed them in the halls. The next several days passed without incident, and although not feeling quite herself, Sarah awoke relieved and clear-headed each morning. She had brought up the idea of getting her driver's license again to her parents, and her mother had offered to take her on Friday. With something to look forward to at the end of the week, days coasted by almost as if in fast forward.

Friday came and went. Sarah passed her written permit test with no trouble, and within the month she expected to be a licensed driver; now she just needed to practice.

Her mother let her drive home from the test and she was surprised how easy it was. She paid meticulous attention to her surroundings, and did not take liberties with speed or signaled instructions. After the 10-mile drive, Sarah felt as if she were old hat behind the wheel, and had actually enjoyed the experience. She again felt a yearning to drive on her own. Knowing that it was actually going to happen allowed her mind to wander into all the possibilities her increased range and accessibility would bring... trips to the mall, exploration of the rural areas bordering Dyersville, following of interesting parties without their knowledge. The world was opening up to her, and it was all due to the confidence she had gained in her ability to handle any situation that arose.

She had not seen her boy since the stare down on the canal trail. Every day she wondered of his whereabouts, his past times, even the uttermost basics- name, age, etc. It was something that was on her mind constantly, but not to the point of distraction... it was just a nice little supplement to her otherwise rigorous regimen of schoolwork, safety, and living under the conventional radar. It felt like she was sneaking ice cream in the middle of the night, or as if she were watching someone inside their home without their knowledge. It was a guilty pleasure that she was gaining more enjoyment from as each day passed.

The week of Andrew's suspension had flown by, and his Monday return weighed heavily on Sarah's mind the weekend before. Would he put the vague 2-and-2 together of her in the archives and his discovery as a plagiarist? The next steps in her planning needed to be laid out, because whether or not he made the connection from the library, she knew high school, and there was no way she would remain anonymous forever. Before he was able to make the discovery, he needed to be taken care of.

Monday came, and sure enough, Andrew came back right along with it. Walking by himself and wearing an old looking jean jacket instead of his usual varsity coat and carrying a backpack that looked stuffed to the gills, he entered the school alone and looked solemn. Watching him nod hello to several passerby's, Sarah followed at a comfortable distance until he turned into 1st period. Not exactly knowing what she was expecting to happen, the complete lack of event that was Andrew's return surprised her, and she even felt the least bit slighted. Does no one care about the integrity of the school paper? Andrew is a *thief*, and although one of intellectual as opposed to physical property, people should treat him as such. Sarah hurried on to her own class, and remained irritatedly curious during it. She had decided she would re-route all day in order to observe Andrew; his treatment of/by others, and any other idiosyncrasies that may arise.

Not one single alarm went off until after 5th period when he went to lunch. Whereas he would usually sit with the jocks, today he had taken company in the group of forlorn students that congregated in the small corridor outside the cafeteria, all clearly waiting for an absence of teachers to light up cigarettes and listen to music out of a small portable radio. The very sight of Andrew conversing with such ilk showed her *(with some relief)* that things were not quite as right as they seemed. Possibly his indiscretions had endeared him to that sort of person? Possibly because of their own treacheries they were more accepting of Andrew's? Regardless, watching the lunch situation brought any thoughts that he had been unaffected by the Journalism incident to an end; quite the contrary. As she expected happened in each and every school in the nation and likely the world, there were certain *"classes"* of people that did not usually mix… what she was witnessing was in effect a small class war-the *"have's"* mingling with the *"have-not's"* under very curious circumstances. Outside of the general curiosity of the events, Sarah was positive that Andrew's teammates on the swim team or his cohorts on the debate squad would certainly frown on him spending his lunch period smoking cigarettes and lurking in the corners with a bunch of likely juvenile delinquents. Knowing the fickle nature of high school friendships *(if only from a 3ʳᵈ party perspective)* she guessed that choosing one would mean, for all intents and purposes, that he was forsaking the other.

II.

Sarah must have zoned out while staring into the corridor because she awoke to the sight of a large boy with dyed black hair slapping the window and giving her the finger. She felt immediately embarrassed, knowing how uncomfortable she would be if someone watched her in captivity. She scurried away quickly, but noticed Andrew looking at her as she did. She did not like or dislike the students that congregated there, but she did feel them to be a bit more dangerous *(and insightful)* than most; making an appearance on their radar, she felt, was a big mistake.

Walking as fast as she could, Sarah wished to travel back in time to the moments before the incident. Making it around the school perimeter in just a few minutes, she found a secluded bench where she ate her lunch and thought long and hard about how to handle the challenging situation she had put herself in. Trying to befriend them would be much too obvious, despite her social prowess, yet ignoring the event altogether was no better an option. Thinking of her as an enemy would lead to discussion, and she felt would imminently lead to Andrew identifying her as his hangman.

Peanut butter and honey on whole grain bread, an apple, water, and a small bag of salted almonds- that is what she ate for lunch, every day. Eating the same things at each meal left one less thing in her life for her to question, one less decision that had to be made in the face of what seemed like an endless pile of them. Food was fuel- enough to keep energy, but not so much to allow body fat or poor digestion. As she finished her lunch, it came to her- she would craft an article for the paper on the pros- and cons- of allowing music in the corridor. It was an issue that got lip service every year, and never reached a firm conclusion. Students didn't see the problem; neither did some faculty, but there were a few sticklers that felt it took the school one dangerous step towards complete anarchy. An even-handed article with a proposed solution and date, should the issue be resolved in the students favor, would win their approval and her invasiveness would be explained. She would ask Mahoney about it in today's class, and write it for next week's edition.

It could be argued that she was making a mountain out of a molehill, but with her plan for Andrew in its' final stages of preparation, no precaution was too thorough. The article will offer her peace of mind, but most importantly will be a solid step towards seamless integration into the student body. No more *fucking* around, she thought, agitated. The gravity and depravity of her plan had briefly dawned on her, and she realized that it will take more than being inconspicuous to avoid scrutiny after it comes to fruition.

III.

Her Monday had felt long, and was as arduous to wind down from as it was to endure. Sarah sat in her room with quiet music as a background, awaiting the arrival of her mother and the beginning of another driving lesson. She was an astute and competent driver after only four practice sessions, and felt more than capable of passing a test on the matter at any time. Today had another focus as well- her mother needed to go to the hardware store in the city for her father *(as un-handy as he was, the coming weekend was to see him attempt a garbage disposal repair)*. Sarah had one piece of shopping to do as well, although not quite as above-the-board. Months of research had led her to a specific brand of petroleum oil used as a cleaner and also found in several art supplies, and a specific mineral oil which she found available at a novelty/candle shop right in the village. Evidence showed that the combining of the two produced a highly flammable, fast-burning compound that was so clean it was almost beyond detection.

She had used the computer in the library for part one of her research on the subject, and had used a coffee shop internet connection for round two. The mineral oil was as common as patchouli or any of the other objectionable scents the hippies in her school drowned themselves in, and she intended to steal the petroleum oil from the hardware store. Three times in the previous month she had taken the bus and walked through the store's aisles, honing a plan that only required an unknowing accomplice... and her mother would certainly do. Unwittingly falling into a daydream about her not-so-imaginary *"friend"* in the black sweatshirt, Sarah was startled and turned beet red when her mother opened her bedroom door. *"Dear, are we driving today? Remember my errand in the city."* Collecting her thoughts she replied *"I had almost forgotten! I was about to go for a walk; I'm glad you caught me."* Sarah's mom shook her head, smiling at the youthful absent-mindedness of her daughter, as farcical as it was.

They were off. The trip was 11 miles each way. It had taken Sarah 30 minutes to get there on the bus, walking the last block, and had taken just 17 minutes to get there today. The prospect of driving on her own was becoming more exciting all the time, and her list of tasks when the time came was already half a page long. They arrived at Gleason's Hardware at approximately quarter to six, and the store was a veritable ghost town. Gleason, presumably, was behind the counter acting busy. Not wanting to waste time searching on her own, her mother effortlessly charmed him out and into an aisle several over from cleaning supplies. Shocked to see another soul, Sarah felt herself glare momentarily at an older woman reading labels on spray cleaner bottles in the aisle she needed to use. Using simple human boundaries as the method of clearing her path, she stood mere inches from the woman, reaching up overhead, and even in front of her in an effort to expedite her product choice. Not a moment after the woman had become uncomfortable and left the scene with a green bottle of Fantastik cleaner did Sarah located the tube she sought. As she had practiced with the toothpaste in her bathroom, she zipped it into the pouch hidden inside the waist of her pants and re-zipped her coat in a matter of seconds. Only one security mirror existed in the store, and with a woman as attractive as her mother commanding his attention, Gleason might as well have been blind. Sarah exited the store, immediately speculating on other situations in which her mother could serve as an unintentional shill. She sat on the steps and waited, no doubt in her mind that she had avoided detection, and excited by the prospect of a drive home in the dark.

IV.

Mahoney loved the idea of resurrecting the music in the corridor story. Sarah had even received a compliment on the timeliness of it, since two students *(little had she known)* had been suspended in the last several weeks for just that type of dastardly insubordination. She was momentarily relieved, and then shocked that she had not considered the fact that she will now have to delve deeper into the belly of the beast for answers. She may in fact be in the corridor at the same time as Andrew, working for the very institution he was unceremoniously but justifiably axed from weeks prior. The smartest and cleanest strategy would certainly be to speak outside the corridor to the students she recognized from within it. Sarah knew it to be a dramatization, but she could not help picture the hostile mob mentality shown on TV when a reporter intervened in an unwelcome situation, and she did not want any part of it.

The two that stuck out the most seemed to be friends, and were as easy to locate as a light in the dark. Swallowing her insecurities, she approached them together towards the end of lunch period at their lockers. *"Hi, my name is Sarah... I don't know either of your names."* *"Uh, yeah. There's a reason for that."* the boy said. As they laughed amongst themselves, Sarah coolly explained *"I write for the school paper... I know it's usually pretty dull, but I wanted to bring up the music in the corridor issue, since it never got handled last year. If we make a good case, I can't see it not getting approved." "Really? We thought you were just going to ask us some stupid questions about homecoming or something. I'm Thomas, and she's Maria. Hello." "It's nice to meet you both..."* Sarah stated, as genuinely as she could muster. They both smelled funny, looked ridiculous, and clearly thought they were better than her. They could die on the spot and she would feel more remorse for the janitor that would likely find their corpses. *"...so, what would you like to state about the music in the corridor issue?"* The boy spoke first. *"Well, everything we do all day here is controlled by someone. Why can't we have 30 minutes of time during our lunch period when we can do what we want? I mean, no one outside the corridor can even HEAR the music." "That's a good point"* Sarah said *"but the counter-point is that the music played out there is vulgar, and therefore it's the school's responsibility to monitor it."* Maria chimed in, intelligently. *"I think the main reason the music out there is vulgar is to get attention so something can be done about it. I think if we were allowed to play music, everyone would be willing to compromise on the content."* Sarah was taken aback by the lucid, logical response given by a girl with black fingernails and a clown on her shirt.

"Thank you guys... I think the article is going to be helpful. It will be out in this Friday's paper. I'm just going to use your first names if that's ok." "Thank you Sarah." said Maria. As they parted, Sarah looked back and saw them speaking about her in what appeared to be a positive light. She even got a quick wave from Thomas. As off-putting as they were, she *had* misjudged them.

Much to her surprise, interviewing the teachers for the article was far more tedious and honestly quite maddening. Ms. Heffernan, Mrs. Joyal, and Mr. Tibbs had been the strongest opposition the previous year, and when Sarah spoke with them today they were no less incensed towards the issue. *"Students are here to learn, not to bring in boom boxes and music at their leisure."* Heffernan barked. *"I agree about the learning"* Sarah stated *"but sometimes it seems like certain students need to express themselves differently."* *"Well I guess there is a time and a place for that, and by my estimation it is when they've either failed or dropped out of Dyersville High."* Heffernan was immediately chastised for the statement by Mr. Tibbs, who was no less opposed to the suggestion of leniency but was far more diplomatic in his approach. *"Sarah, although there are probably plenty of students that could handle the situation maturely, there are many others that when given an inch, will take a mile. We can't set the example that with a little bit of student unrest, they can have anything they want."* Just to make sure her cantankerous point was made clear, Heffernan chimed *"It's the parents that pay our salaries, not you students. Until you're paying us from your hard-earned paycheck, we'll do what we want."* Sarah thanked them for their time, and left abruptly. The good-natured, middle-of-the-road article she had originally envisioned was not going to be possible. Much to her dismay, she felt that two bizarrely dressed outcasts had conveyed a better case *(and certainly a more considerate one)* than two decorated members of the faculty. She had never been in one of Heffernan's classes, and she found herself very thankful. A more objectionable person she had not encountered in some time.

After clearing the students and teachers remarks with Mr. Mahoney, she began her story. Mahoney shook his head when reading over the transcripts of Heffernan's statements, but did not tell Sarah to change or omit them. She wanted to commend his integrity on the matter, knowing that he will catch hell for it later, but she did not. He surely knew what he was in for, and it wouldn't be the first time.

Her story was thorough- she had gone through the last two stories the paper had run on the issue, borrowed any relevant facts, and pieced together her version. She had opened the story with a quote from Heffernan; this was geared both to elicit response, and also to get the negative out of the way first. She was taught that to finish on your strongest point is the most effective strategy. There was also a part of her that was anxious to have everyone in the school read Heffernan's statements in disgust. No matter which side of the issue you stood on, the things she said were unnecessary. Sarah ended with the comments from Maria, and a sentence that read *"High School is a time of expression, learning, and maturity. Hopefully the faculty and the student body can work together to honor those tenets."* The story was finished, edited, and turned in.

Now she would wait.

Grievances from the paper usually reared their heads the Monday after the Friday morning release; Most were so petty and forgettable that it took a weekend of reflection for anyone to even formulate anything to complain about. Much to Sarah's surprise, it was the beginning of 3rd period Friday that her buzz began. First were looks of approval from students she had never spoken with or even condescended to look at… next were looks of confusion from faculty, and the proverbial icing on the cake came in the form of her first ever call out of class to the principal's office. She knew that the only way she would actually be in trouble is if she had printed something Mahoney had told her not to. Since that was not the case, she was anxious but not worried during her mid-period walk of shame. Students towards the end of their high school careers were still not above the *"ooohhh's"* and *"aaaahhh's"* when someone was called out of class, and receiving that kind of attention left

Sarah feeling very uneasy and visible. Possibly the meeting was to discuss the music issue- possibly it had been resolved as a result of her story?

Possible, but unlikely. As a realist, and a quite pessimistic one at that, she was much more certain that there was some type of trouble afoot and that she was somehow involved. 10 steps left to her destination. Sarah flipped the switch, smiling disarmingly as she checked in with the principal's secretary.

V.

"And who are you, dear?" "I'm Sarah Bidding. I was sent for out of my 3rd period history class to see Mr. Carlson." Putting her sausage fingers to work, the secretary tried to find a paper trail on Sarah's arrival. *"Oh! You're the girl from the paper! Dear, I haven't seen Ms. Heffernan this upset in the entire 10 years I've worked here... you watch out for yourself in there."* Hmm... Heffernan. Not a problem Sarah was expecting, but certainly not inconceivable.

Mr. Mahoney was in the room as well, which was quite a surprise. As soon as Carlson had opened the door and beckoned her in she had felt that something was not quite right, and Mahoney's presence provided stark confirmation. Heffernan was sitting in a beautiful leather and dark wood armchair, legs crossed, and a scowl on her puckered face that would have spoiled milk. Mahoney looked despondent... not a look that she would expect from the only teacher in the entire school she both liked for his personality and respected for his integrity.

Carlson looked like the bored, lethargic pig that she always thought him to be. There was no charisma to him. No charm, no magnetism. Nothing. How he became Principal in a well-to-do school like Dyersville had puzzled Sarah often. Surely a quiet, pretty, stable town could have their pick of educators and administrators; even more surely he was not the pick of *any* litter.

Sarah was instructed by finger point to sit in a black folding chair that faced the group. Mahoney was off to her right; Heffernan and Carlson were front and center. Mahoney spoke first, and was almost instantly interrupted. *"Sarah, I'm sorry that you're here right now…"* Carlson cut him off at the pass and droned. *"This meeting is to discuss your article in the paper this morning. Are you aware of the problem we have?"* Very nice, Sarah noticed. Psychology 101- ask the question of the questioned to see if they'll hang themselves- another amateurish display that made her an even harsher critic of Carlson.

"Oh, I'm very aware of it. The students talk about it at lunch all the time. No one really understands why music can't be played…" Heffernan could no longer contain herself. *"NOT the issue with the MUSIC… the ISSUE with your ARTICLE!"* she barked. Mahoney blurted out *"BARBARA!"* as if to silence her or at least distract her from the glare she had placed on Sarah. The harder she glared, the more comfortable Sarah felt. She felt that she could break Heffernan… make her do or say something so inappropriate that she would HAVE to be held accountable. She continued, unfazed by Mahoney's intervention. *"The PROBLEM is that you can't just take quotes out of CONTEXT and use them to DEFAME a well-respected educator. You know as well as I do that I DID NOT say those things that you printed!"* *"Of course you did, Ms. Heffernan."* Sarah asserted in her soft, yet most confident tone. *"I have the Dictaphone tape of our entire conversation."* Sarah was young, but was a student of her craft. She knew that her word was only as good as that of a 17-

year old girl, so any time she intended to quote in a story, she taped it and transcribed it later. This instance was no different.

Mahoney gave her a sly grin, which for obvious reasons she did not return, however with this new discovery she could not imagine the conversation going on much longer. *"How DARE you… tape me without my expressed consent. Who do you think you are?"* Heffernan was desperate, and it was showing. *"I addressed myself as a member of the school paper and told you exactly what my article was to cover. Anything you told me after that I am within my rights to use."* This factual statement must have come across as indignant to both of the idiots sitting across from her, because they looked at each other as if given a cue to defend themselves.

Carlson moaned *"Sarah, this is less of an issue of what you think you can and can't do, and more of one about respecting your elders and the faculty at this school. Ms. Heffernan obviously did not mean what she said in your interview, if it indeed happened the way you said, and now those erroneous statements have damaged her reputation. What do you think we should do about that?"* Sarah thought to herself briefly about the question, and about her *actual* answer. Instead she gave *"I think that we should put something specific in the paper regarding privacy rights, also mentioning the fact that if you agree to talk to someone writing an article, what you say may be used without further permission. I guess I see how that could be misunderstood."* Diplomacy in situations like this was beyond difficult, but was also beyond necessary. Any wavering right now would be disastrous. *"I meant what should we do about what you've done."* said Carlson. *"I guess I don't understand sir, what have I done?"* as Sarah uttered the statement, Mahoney's hand went to his forehead. He saw the curve ball a few seconds before Sarah. *"Sarah, you have defamed a respected member of this faculty, and compromised her reputation to thousands of people."*

"But Mr. Carlson, I just transcribed exactly what she said and used it for my article."

"Sarah, that is NOT all you did. Ms. Heffernan did not mean those things, and we cannot set a precedent of this type of misuse of the school paper." Carlson paused, and Sarah stayed quiet, since anything else that came out of her mouth was not going to be helpful. *"We have chosen to suspend you for two days. I'm sorry it had to work out like this, but hopefully this will be a valuable lesson about your responsibility as a journalist."* Sarah was speechless. Mahoney was not.

"Steve! You CANNOT suspend my student for writing the truth in our school paper. She has the TAPE for god's sake... let's listen to it together!" *"That will not be necessary. I don't want to give this thing any longer legs than it already has. We can write the suspension up as sick days so it doesn't appear on her transcripts, but besides that, the decision is final."*

The look on Heffernan's face was so arrogant and childish that it took all the restraint Sarah had in her being not to pull the disguise off the end of her writing pen and shove the blade in her throat. It took all her concentration to not show it. Not a blink, not a wavering of her facial expression. She set her stare through the back of Heffernan's head, and thought back to the teaching of Sun Tzu in *"The Art of War"*. The enemy must at no time, no matter the gravity of your distress, know that you are in distress. Sarah was devastated, but no one in the room knew it. She would find a fitting channel for the pain she was feeling right now, and the very idea brought her a moment of peace.

CHAPTER VII.

It had been decided that in the interest of making her suspension seem like sick days, it would be delayed until Thursday and Friday of the following week. Mahoney had told her that they did not want it to seem like she was being suspended on the eve of the release of the paper- They didn't want what they called a *"witch hunt"*, with students and faculty alike deducing that a student had in fact been suspended for performing above-the-board journalism. High schools rally around such things, and if discovered, the position that Carlson and Heffernan took would not hold up to any level of scrutiny. They had even gone so far as to ask Mahoney to mention to Sarah that this was a private matter and should not be discussed amongst her peers, or even addressed with her guidance counselor. Mahoney was shaking while addressing Sarah, and she felt much worse for him than she did for herself. He was feeling like he had let down his biggest fan, and was also obviously questioning his loyalties, and the merits of them. The only mistake Mahoney had made was in assuming that living with ethics, morals, and high standards of integrity entitles you to be treated by others in kind. The phrase *'disappointed, not surprised'* ran through Sarah's mind often, and this was a stellar example. She was a guiltless victim- punished for following orders by people too weak minded to deal with any level of self-truth.

The truth that Sarah was focusing on right now was her desire to leave the school in disarray when she walked out on Wednesday afternoon for her unexpected and unwanted 4-day weekend. She had felt like she was waiting for a precise moment to carry out her next project and was now grateful for the clarity; the moment would be Tuesday during 5th period lunch. She wanted a day or so to exist in the chaos; to take in the pain, confusion, and anguish that would be felt by all. Rarely do emotions run so high that they feel like an actual living entity, and she predicted that the waves of sorrow crashing through the school on that day would be palpable. She wanted to feel what they were feeling... maybe if enough of them felt it at once, it would wash over her and bring her heart to life. She *wanted* to be devastated... she *wanted* to feel like screaming, crying, and throwing up all at the same time. Sarah knew these things existed, but no situation yet in her life had allowed her to touch them with her own hands.

Tuesday had come so rapidly it was almost as if the weekend had not existed. The only proof that Monday had lived is that she had phoned in and gotten an appointment to take her driver's license test... one of the only perks of her days off was that she was now available for a morning appointment; Friday, 10:45am. By 11:30am, Sarah would be a licensed driver.

Her project checklist this morning was long... almost too long. Even with waking up 45 minutes early, she was double and triple checking mere minutes before her scheduled departure.

- ➤ Lip gloss bottle with liquid #1
- ➤ Nail polish bottle with liquid #2
- ➤ Empty nail polish bottle for mixing
- ➤ Swizzle sticks
- ➤ Cotton balls
- ➤ Hand sanitizer
- ➤ Clean bandana
- ➤ Small rubber case
- ➤ Extra shirt
- ➤ Extra pants
- ➤ Rubber surgical gloves
- ➤ Headphones
- ➤ *The Poems of Emily Dickinson*
- ➤ Folding knife
- ➤ Special pen
- ➤ Copies of last week's school paper

Every item accounted for and packed neatly into her backpack, Sarah blasted out the door two minutes off schedule, but with still more than enough time to make the first bell.

Her mind was clear… she had thought this up and down, forward and backwards, dozens of times over. The walk to school was a time for relaxation and reflection- Andrew deserved to be in the position he is in right now, and should Sarah not be the messenger, surely society would have shown him in another way. She put her headphones on and stuck the cord in her pocket. They muted the surrounding noise nicely, and would also inhibit any casual conversations that may have arisen between home and school. This was a weighty time, and although Sarah was confident and well-prepared, she could not afford petty distractions.

Sarah stood at the announcement board from the minute she

arrived at school until she saw Andrew arrive through the doors and make his way to homeroom. He was wearing the same denim jacket he had been wearing since returning from suspension, and she had been counting on it. The weather was clear and quite cool and although the forecast called for rain, the weather station her father was watching prior to her departure said it would likely hold off until afternoon. 5th period lunch ran between 10:33am and 11:13am, and Sarah had acquired a library pass the previous week so she would not be bound to study hall during it. Logistically, she was set. If all went as planned it should take no more time than walking to and from class to complete her task.

2nd period was Health class, and aside from being tediously boring and just as simple, it was also the easiest class to secure a bathroom pass. One of the few benefits she had found in being a girl was that no one ever questioned why you were taking a bag. She left on her excursion with bag in tow, and knew she had less than 10 minutes to work with. Locked in a stall, she unpacked her kit and went to it- gloves on, she carefully stood the bottles on the small shelf located at waist level inside the stall door. When the liquids mixed in her tests, it created a grayish yogurt-like substance; she mixed equal parts, stirred and shook, and sure enough the results had duplicated. Once she was sure, she put the remainder of each liquid in the toilet, along with her gloves and the swizzle sticks. The new bottle was wrapped carefully in a bandana and secured inside a small rubber case usually reserved for a manicure set. Seven minutes.

II.

4th period had ended before Sarah had even acknowledged its beginning, and she made for the door with cautious haste. In every lunch period she had observed, Andrew would leave his jacket and bag at his new lunch seat in the corner by the corridor, and then brave the lunch line. Usually about nine minutes to get lunch, 15 to eat, and the rest to fraternize in the corridor, Sarah placed the timeline for her finale right around 11am. Upon approaching the lunchroom she spotted Andrew and was relieved to see him heading for the corner. She had placed copies of the newspaper on his table between 3rd and 4th period, and in the only part of her plan left to chance, they were still there now. He glanced briefly at the paper, hung his coat, and jumped in line. Sarah performed her ritual three breaths and started to walk… she had already freed the bottle from its hiding place, and was holding it in her right hand. The bustle at the beginning of the lunch period could have concealed a small riot, so drawing attention to herself was not her primary worry. She must not delay too long reaching the library- unaccounted for minutes could be a liability. Upon reaching Andrew's table, she bent to look at the paper, uncapped the nail polish bottle, and poured the grey liquid as thoroughly as she could around the cuff and left sleeve of his jacket, ending at the neckline. Just as she had hoped, it was barely noticeable, and she had managed to be so as well.

Tightly re-capping the bottle, she turned to leave and was met within a few steps by Maria- the girl she had interviewed for her article. *"Sarah!"* *"Hi Maria… how are you?"* *"I'm ok… I really liked your article. Did you get in trouble for that?"* Patience wearing thin already, Sarah managed *"A little… nothing big. Just doing my job, I guess."* Maria approached and obviously wanted to talk. Sarah asserted *"Unless I want to get in more, I have to go… I just stopped in here to drop a note with a friend. See you?"* *"Yeah"* Maria pined, *"…thanks for including me in the article."* Anything more abrupt would have left Maria feeling put off... the two-minute delay was costly, but not nearly as much so as appearing suspicious. As soon as she left the fluorescent yellow confines of the cafeteria she broke into an all-out sprint; good behavior and exemplary attendance afforded her the luxury of a few minutes here and there with many teachers, and she was hoping today would be the same. The librarian checked her pass and mentioned the few minutes with a coy smile. She knew and liked Sarah, and surely did not think twice as she tossed the pass in the trash and made no note of the arrival time.

Positioning herself at a table facing the hall and with her back to the check-in desk, she sanitized her hands, sanitized the bottle inside and out, wrapped it back up in the bandana, and zipped it into the pouch. She had sewn a secret compartment in the bottom of her bag, and now with mission complete, the case was stashed safely inside it. In the incredibly unlikely event that her bag was searched, and the even less likely possibility that the secret compartment was found, it would take an exhaustive set of lab tests to determine that anything but nail polish had existed in the small glass bottle.

It was now 10:56am, and Sarah could see on the counter that the girls' lavatory pass was available. She walked up and signed it out, smiled at the student working the desk, and made her way into the hall. At an Olympic pace, she walked directly to the cafeteria hallway and stood out of sight at the corner nearest the corridor. She could not see Andrew- he was not at his seat, nor was his jacket, and he was not in the corridor. Her heart rate elevated, and even though she had been breathing consciously and remained relaxed all day, her mind started to run the worst-case scenarios. Had he discovered the liquid?

Had he seen her? Had he been called to the office…?

Mere moments after the thoughts had entered her head, Andrew walked less than a foot from her, presumably returning from the boys' room. Almost as if acting on Sarah's will, he walked through the cafeteria, scooped up his bag, and entered the corridor. She had four minutes left on her lavatory pass, and had started to come to the realization that she may have miscalculated. She looked at her watch, ran her hand through her hair, and looked back towards the corridor at the precise second that a boy with a leather coat and dog tags sneakily held a lighter out to Andrew's cigarette. What happened next was beyond anything Sarah, or anyone else in the vicinity, could have ever imagined.

Like the tail of a comet, the liquid on Andrew's sleeve pulled the flame towards it. Time seemed to stop, and the only two faces she was able to view were Andrew's and the boy with the lighter, and both looked curiously confused… but only for a brief moment. When the flame and the liquid finally met face to face, Andrew's arm went up with such fury it looked as if to be in fast forward. Confusion turned to horror as the fire danced and flickered, and Andrew began to shake. The flame raced up the sleeve, caught the cigarette, and within what couldn't have been two seconds had engulfed Andrew's head, face, and entire upper torso.

People were running around the corridor not knowing which way was up… it was full blown chaos, and the only certainty is that no one was helping extinguish the flames. The fire alarm eventually went, but by this time Andrew had flailed his way into a corner and was on the ground with his arms in the air. The one do-gooder in the entire group started grabbing drinks off all the trays and splashing them on the flames, but it yielded no result. If help did not arrive immediately, Andrew would be burned to a crisp. Thick black smoke billowed from the corner, and Sarah was mesmerized by the colors the heat was turning the glass. She could not pull her eyes away from it… and she was not alone. There were dozens of students in the hallway watching a boy burn to death as if it were a plot twist in a television show.

Frightening in and of itself was the fact that not a soul had yet made a true attempt at help.

There were several students standing speechless and overcome inside the corridor… most were hunched over, their faces shrouded by hands or coats. Two girls were embracing each other and crying hysterically; it all seemed rather disingenuous to Sarah, as there was still no stab at a rescue. Teachers had begun to make their way to the scene- prior to that, the only adults present were the cafeteria staff and they were certainly not going to risk their lives for one of a group that they had surely come to despise. Sarah often wondered how close any member of that staff had ever been to succumbing to the temptation to poison the whole herd. Watching the droves of ungrateful, disrespectful teenagers day in and day out could surely bring an otherwise rational person within inches of drastic measures.

There was supposed to be at least one faculty member supervising each lunch period, and in fates' twist that favored the completion of Sarah's project, today there was not. The teachers that did arrive were almost as useless as the students- looking at each other for answers, shuffling around in the *"action"* position *(partially squatted down, arms out, head roving back and forth like a gun turret)...* but no real action to speak of. Andrew had been burning *(and screaming)* for probably close to two minutes, and Sarah knew that much longer would cause death from carbon monoxide poisoning or suffocation.

Finally Mr. Novak- the health teacher- came rushing in with a blanket and started attacking Andrew with it. His pants caught fire, but he paid no mind and continued his rescue campaign as if possessed. He had succeeded in putting out some of the flames when in a grotesque twist Andrew's body fell forward, leaving mounds of burned flesh and matter on the corridor wall and giving the dwindling flames new life. Novak could no longer ignore his own peril, and turned the blanket on himself. As the teacher put out the flame on his leg it became apparent to the scores watching that Andrew was dead. His body was crumpled into a sub-human shape, and was face down in the short grass surrounding the perimeter of the corridor. Impossible not to stare at was the burned human form left on the coarse cement wall. The denim jacket that had served as Andrew's death cloak was amongst the burned remains, but there were also clearly identifiable portions of human hair and skull, and what appeared to be part of a hand.

Several people had fainted at this point, and the area had become a swarm of misdirected chaos. No one knew what to do. Fire engines approached, albeit far too late, and eventually even Carlson made his softheaded way down to the scene; obvious from the moment he arrived was that nothing in his sheltered, privileged life had even partially prepared him for what he witnessed. His knees quaked and a hand shot to his mouth as if to prevent him from vomiting. He took one step in reverse, stumbled over a backpack, and came to rest against a row of lockers. His guise of leadership was shattered, and he crept back towards the halls as quickly as he had arrived. She had broken him; it was not something she expected as a fringe benefit of Andrew's elimination, but it was a welcome one. Carlson would never be the same, and Sarah had witnessed his undoing first hand.

The firemen had arrived along with an ambulance, and the only teacher that had risen to the occasion, Novak, was still in the thick of it. They had covered the body, and began looking around probingly for some sign of what had led to the horror strewn at their feet. Several students had begun talking to the firemen and soon after to a newly-arrived police detective. The boy that held out the lighter was talked to, consoled, and let go. His lighter was examined- amazing that in the midst of such a commotion he still held on to it- but it was no more useful a clue than the cigarette Andrew had intended to smoke.

No one's whereabouts were specifically accounted for the rest of the day- Sarah headed back to the library some 40 minutes after leaving to retrieve her things, and was not questioned in the halls or on her way in or on her way out of the library. The school was paralyzed.

III.

"Attention." The voice demanded over the loud speaker. Carlson was the usual announcement speaker, and though the voice was not identifiable as anyone specific, it was certainly not his. *"Due to the accident in the lunchroom corridor, classes are dismissed for the remainder of the day. Any student with any information regarding the situation is encouraged to visit the main office immediately."*

The usual confusion that followed a surprise announcement was all but forgone, and replacing it was a zombie-like exodus from the rear doors of the school. Those that had not seen had certainly heard- a student burning to death during lunch *(while surrounded by dozens of people)* left a profound feeling of vulnerability that had everyone wanting out. There would be plenty of time for discussion, plenty of time for reflection on the tragic end to an oh-so-promising young life… but today, avoidance, denial, hiding, and confusion. Very little eye contact was made between students as they all left as quickly as they could. Sarah strolled behind, observing the stark differences in mannerisms and interaction that had occurred in the course of just an hour and a half. Several students were seated in front of their lockers with faces in their hands, and as it must have advised in the crisis control handbook, there were handfuls of teachers walking among them aggressively offering support. Within 10 minutes, the school was a virtual ghost town. Those that remained did so in complete silence; to hear a high school that housed almost a thousand students on any given day fall hush was truly eerie, even to Sarah.

The next morning was no less odd. The attendance rate was at 60%, Sarah had learned- nearly 18% lower than the worst attendance rate ever recorded in Dyersville High School history. Classes were half full of the same zombie-like creatures that exited the school the previous afternoon. Sarah could not help but think that this is what it must have been like in the old frontier days when typhoid or small pox or some other now-curable killer struck a village. *What would Laura Ingalls do?* she wondered, momentarily amusing herself. Her parents had offered her the out today as well, but she chose to attend, and chose to walk. She did so with hesitation so as to not seem brazen, but her parents did not seem surprised at her decision; Even though their communication was often sparse, her resoluteness and responsibility were unquestioned.

The day was filled with teachers trying their best to elicit some level of interest in students, and students pretending to have any. Sarah was sure that after consideration the rest of the week would be written off in terms of grading, attendance, and anything else that would blemish a student's record. The situation truly existed outside parameters that either the school or an individual could grasp or cope with. There had been one suicide when Sarah was a sophomore, and it was a mildly turbulent time, but did not even hold a candle to the unrest occurring now. She was one period away from Journalism *(which was the only thing she looked forward to all day)*, and at this point had counted four students crying uncontrollably in the halls, and another three simply sitting in the stairwells looking as if they had overdosed on sedatives. The faculty, on the contrary, were hustling and rushing around feverishly trying to attend to all the now-damaged goods... she had been approached several times and asked if she needed to speak with someone regarding her feelings on the events of the previous day. She replied *"No, thank you"* and did so with a forlorn yet composed look, which sent the do-gooders on to more vulnerable subjects.

Mahoney looked as if he had not slept in days. On the eve of Sarah's troubling suspension, he now had to deal with the untimely death of a student that he had ousted from his class not a month prior. He was undoubtedly thinking that the one situation had in some way led to the other. Sarah wanted to console him; assure him that Andrew had paved his own way and that he had been nothing but a positive influence on him. Even with the trust and confidence she had in her interpersonal abilities she thought such a conversation would be risky. Mahoney was sharp, and in this heightened state, any inkling that she may be speaking from any position of not-so-common knowledge would be disastrous.

There were three people in Journalism that day. Sarah did not initiate conversation with Mr. Mahoney, however she made herself open to it and he responded. His distress was unconcealable, both in appearance and voice. *"Sarah, I wanted to say again how sorry I am about your suspension. It is truly one of the most inappropriate things I have ever witnessed as an educator, and I feel more than a little responsible."* Sarah replied as she felt any student with feelings or a moral compass would. *"Mr. Mahoney, it was not your fault, and in light of the other things going on, is not even worth talking about right now. I am so sorry about Andrew. I know I spoke with you about his story, but that doesn't mean…"* Mahoney interrupted immediately, seeing her statement leading to a potential emotional outburst. *"Sarah, the two things are completely unrelated… I do not want you to speak of them, or even think of them, together. You did the right thing in regards to the story he stole. This other thing… well… it is just an unfortunate tragedy."*

Sarah looked at the floor and manufactured a relieved yet exhausted look when her eyes returned to his. *"Thank you. I know you must be struggling with it too, and I hope you can see it the same way you've told me to."* Mahoney's eyes actually teared up, and he looked very grateful for the sentiment. *"Sarah, I want you to know how much I value your insight and contributions to this class. I will assure as Mr. Carlson mentioned that these days do not go on your transcript. In fact, I think you should look at them as days off for a job well done."* Mahoney produced a weak, sarcastic grin. Sarah smiled meekly, and thought devilishly about the prospect of a reward system for the completion of her *"projects"*. A job well done indeed… though never in her natural life would accolades come her way for completing the kind of job she took the most pride in.

IV.

Her driving instructor was the kind of person that appeared destined for the thankless, monotonous job life had handed him. A meek and scrawny 40-something with a large, oddly grown mustache and messy hair, he handled the instruction portion of the test as if he were reading off a cue card somewhere in the distance. Sarah felt she could have been wearing a bear suit and holding a severed head and he would have paid no mind. She was over-prepared for her test, and if anything, she thought the drone may appreciate the meticulousness of her preparation.

Sarah followed every order given swiftly and accurately, and any curve ball she handled seamlessly. She had read pages and pages of online forums concerning driving tests and very much felt she had read about every trick in the book. The test lasted all of 15 minutes and no eye contact had been made the entire time. Upon exiting the car, the instructor said *"You did a truly excellent job. It is rare these days to encounter someone that has prepared."* Sarah bid him thank you, his eyes still not meeting hers. She had received 100% on her test, brought it inside and showed her mother, and then drove home- all the while daydreaming about the new adventures she would soon be embarking on. She had the weekend ahead of her, and intended to make use of it in her newly liberated capacity… the mall, the outskirts of town that walking did not favor, and a search… for her boy.

He had been invisible since their canal path encounter, but had been a constant presence in Sarah's mind. Still unconvinced that the sightings were of a random sort, she was left in a constant state of wonder as to how, why… and most simply, *who* the stranger was that had entered her life in such overt and also such subtle fashions. Flashing back to the incident at the mall made her feel warm, and intensified her desire to begin the hunt.

There were more than a few mentions on the local news of the situation at Dyersville High. In true local news form, the lack of real or conclusive information regarding the events led to almost comical conjecture and hyperbole- one news report actually tried to link the fire to the lack of stringent enough production standards in overseas clothing factories. It asserted that the chemicals were *so* potent in the dyeing of the denim Andrew was wearing that they provided a combustible environment, thus leading to his demise. Another had pieced together a short expose' on the quality of cafeteria food, the serving of it on Styrofoam plates, and... global warming. It amazed Sarah that these assassins of true intellect could even keep straight faces during their laughable presentations. Her father felt the same, and it actually created an interesting few minutes of interaction between them. As soon as she got the feeling her father was going to start asking how the healing process was going, she exited. It was upstairs to make a list of destinations and then back down later to attempt to borrow the car.

She felt a deep sense of safety and a settling air of relaxation in her room. It was neither large nor extravagant, but it contained the things she valued most in the world, and offered the only true privacy she ever felt. Even when walking alone down the canal path well after dark there was always the feeling of invasiveness... no matter the hour, or the obscurity of the route, Sarah existed in every waking moment outside her room as if there were someone watching. She immediately laid down on the floor and stared up at the ceiling full of glow-in-the-dark stars. It was just enough past dusk that they had started to come alive; charged by the bright sun of the day, they now illuminated her hiding place and gave permission for her to indulge her imagination. Sleep fell over her just moments later; she was deep in paradoxical thought, both fantasizing about the next surprise encounter with the one she sought, and rerunning Andrew's grotesque final moments from Tuesday's 5th period lunch. At that moment neither felt any more real than the other, and both seemed as distant as the stars in the sky.

CHAPTER VIII.

Simon stabbed the man swiftly in all the vital organs, just as the knife fighting diagrams he had studied had illustrated. He was shocked at how much force it truly took to push the blade through flesh and tissue, even with this intensity. The sense of panic that had been present moments ago had diminished, and now that the man was surely dead the only worry left was escape. The last bus back to Dyersville left in 15 minutes and he was at least that in walking distance from the station. If he got stuck in the city overnight his chances of being caught increased exponentially. He had to get out, and he had to do it now.

He found a plastic bag on the street, took his bloodied shirt, jacket, and knife, and wrapped them up inside it as if he were on his way home with groceries. The sight of a thin teenage boy walking around with no coat on in this weather might raise an eyebrow or two, but being cold or appearing irresponsible were not 25-to-life-type infractions. Securing his keys and tying his shoes tight, he began the run to the bus station as if being chased. As long as the bus didn't leave early, he would make it. He *had* to.

With the blinking front light signaling two minutes until departure, Simon paid the $2.40 fee with the last three dollars he had. The sweat that covered his arms and face felt as if it had frozen solid as soon as his movement had come to a stop. He thought of the warmth of the coat contained in his grocery bag, but even in the hazy light cast by the dull street lamp in the alley he could tell that it was decorated with more than a speck or two of blood. Discomfort was not unusual to him. He welcomed it… even engineered it. He had an ongoing and profound feeling that his previous life of privilege and comfort had made him weak and easy prey for society's vultures. Comfort was afforded to him in spades throughout his entire life; in fact, it was almost as if allowing anything *but* would have been a punishable offense. At the hand of parents, grandparents- Simon was afforded all anyone could ever want… but want it he did not.

As soon as his mind had begun to see its own way, the methodology that had been employed to raise him into a societal standout began to erode. The things he felt inside were not pride in work well-done or confidence in character well-built. He felt alienated, alone, and bitter… not at one single person but towards himself, and towards a culture that professed *this* as the true measure of success. His grades, his team accomplishments, medals, commendations…the purpose behind them had seemed so clear, and he had been so wrapped up in their procurement, that never had he thought to question the merit of the path itself.

As he started to chip away at his so recently solid foundations, the loneliness and discontent crashed in like a tidal wave. The outlets for his internal pain became self-induced physical pain and a then-yet unrequited desire to hurt others. He would fabricate stories of how he had been injured when questioned by school administrators… cuts received running through brush, bruises received in a friendly wrestling match between floor mates. 14 years old was too young to be put in a captive environment with such a questioning mind. Those that existed seamlessly were those ingrained with the desires to excel in their directed pastimes, practices, and rigmarole, and had no basis or inkling to waiver from the path. He watched them- all day, every day- and was in some part jealous of their neutrality and their complacence with a situation that was making him as sad, lonely, and abandoned as he felt it humanly possible to bear.

The man in the alley several years later was not simply fodder for his imagination, but more a confirmation as to the depths that his fantasy mind would let itself integrate into reality. While the man had indeed brought fate upon himself, neither appearance nor demeanor could have given clue that he had selected a target apt to mirror his own hostility. Simon was walking in the city as he often did with no reverence for personal safety or concern for locale; the alley he found trouble in was certainly not surprised to see it- it was a known drug trading spot, and even that night Simon had seen at least two prostitutes and one man that he thought to be dead, half covered in trash and laying in a distorted way on the ground. It was a cut-through between a coffee shop that he frequented and a small used bookstore that carried late night hours. Neither were in fantastic parts of town, but the winding roads between them were the true hazard. Most, even by car, would choose to go down Elm to Atlantic and follow the perimeter of the freeway. The cut across- Anderson- was essentially a local road. Simon's mindset was that if he acted like he belonged there- as if him walking down the alley was as right as a December snow- he would not be hassled or even acknowledged.

He studied the racial minority in an area very specifically- when he saw a large group of men together, he always looked to see who was the odd man out, and scrutinized his behavior. It was always a mix of cool bravado and acute awareness. Anything more overt would certainly provoke interest, and anything meeker would certainly out him as the black sheep. They were behavior traits that Simon took with him on each trip to the city and he had not yet been wrong about their protective powers. Until tonight, he existed like a ghost amongst the chaos he wandered through; it took a doped-up Hispanic man making the mistake of thinking he had stumbled on to an easy target to change... everything.

II.

"Hey kid, get over here." Simon had heard the order, but was neither going to acknowledge or obey. *"Yo homey, did you hear me? Get over here kid."* Simon went in to alert mode and did a gear check. Trouble may have finally found him, and should it be more than a bluff, he would be ready. He had been ready every day and every minute, in wake or in sleep, since he had been attacked during the night at school. He had sworn to himself that he would never be taken advantage of again; the school attack marked the onset of his tornado of blame, and while harshest on himself, the rest was cast towards those he fingered as making him weak and unprepared for the perils that life hid. He carried two blades at all times- one folded in

his front pocket and concealed by a handkerchief, and one small fixed-blade knife either in the back of his pants or dangling from a thick string around his neck... weather depending. He also had eight links of ¼ inch steel chain attached to the end of his wallet and affixed with a heavy steel clip to his belt. Those were the items on his person- had he had his backpack, the inventory list would lengthen.

Still unresponsive and walking uninterrupted, the tone of the man changed one last time before interaction was inevitable. "Hey *motherfuckerrr... are you ignoring me on purpose, or do you have a problem?*" *"No problem sir."* Simon said sternly, not making eye contact or even diverting his eyes from the path ahead. A peripheral glance showed the man approaching from the side. They were 10 yards from a small lit patch of alley, and that is where Simon had determined he would make his stand. *"Oh then you little prick, you were just ignoring me on purpose... hey... FUCK YOU."* Breathing deeply, Simon held fast to the idea that he was still being strongly underestimated, and that he would use that to his advantage. They approached the lit patch and Simon slowed, turned sheepishly towards his stalker, and put his hands up unassumingly. *"Man, I don't have a problem. I don't have any money, I'm just passing through."* *"Passing through? You don't get to just pass through, little man..."* The man spoke in just above a whisper, obviously as an intimidation technique. *"This is not the suburbs homey. You don't just get to be here like it's yours..."* With that the man approached Simon, trying to divert his glance down the alley by looking past him, and he grabbed at Simon's coat. Simon turned away, batting the arm down and throwing his hood back in one rapid motion. *"Kid, you had better just give me your fuckin' money... this is not a fight you want to be in..."* The last statement was true. The location was sketchy, the footing was rough, and the light was dim. Fuck it. Nothing can be done about it now. If he were to run, he could never walk down the alley again, or he would be caught by the man's friends at the next intersection.

The man grabbed at his coat again, and this time Simon let him attach for a brief moment... just long enough to extract a blade and shove in into the man's' elbow. *"OOOoooohhhh... you motherfucker... now you're FUCKED!"* The man drew a short fixed blade knife and Simon knew he had better finish what he started while the man was still writhing from the wound to his arm. Using his own diversion against him Simon peered down the alley, waited for the man to look, and thrust a blade strongly into his lower abdomen across the body from the weapon. The man pawed at Simon with the blade and Simon cut across the weaponed arm with a savage downward slash causing the knife to tumble to the ground. The man fumbled in his coat for another weapon and Simon used the moment to grab him and thrust the knife through and across his neck, keeping the weakening body at arm's length through a strong grip on a handful of hair. Now gurgling and no longer a threat, Simon used the adrenaline stored through years of fantasy, frustration, and anticipation to put the man down for good. He thrust through what he knew to be the liver, lungs, and heart. Leaving no stone unturned, he finished with a lateral laceration down each wrist, and even in the few seconds he had been working, the man had surely bled out and died. No one remained in the alley with the exception of the trash-covered man, and he had surely not seen a thing. Simon's vision was crisp, his senses were heightened. He felt as if for the first time in his life he *deserved* to be in that alley, and was not just telling himself so.

III.

The bus ride back to Dyersville felt like the longest, least eventful movie man had ever created. It felt like a dream state, however there was a powerful sense of let-down and disappointment in knowing that nothing yet to happen tonight, or any night soon, could ever rival what he had just done and how he had just felt. He felt now, sitting motionless and freezing in a ripped bus seat, as if he were radiating light, or energy, or *something*, and wondered if the people standing idle on the streets could see it through the bus windows. The only feeling he could even remotely relate it to was when he first began to drink coffee… drinking enough of it could make him feel a sense of elation that seemed unrivaled by any other stimulus, and unreachable with any mere human pleasure or comfort. The feeling had lessened over time, but at its beginning was a sense of power and heightened awareness uniquely similar to what he now felt. The paradox in the manners he had reached those feelings provided a much-needed mood lightener. Almost home… walking through the crisp night back to his house would be the usual relaxing, uneventful endeavor that it always was, and the calm would be welcomed. Though the bus ride was only 25 minutes, it had given him time to absorb what had happened, and he now felt physically weak and sleepy. Just as his eyes started to flutter his stop was called and he once again made his way into the night. One more mile and a day that had opened the door to the rest of his life would end as quietly as it began. Asleep alone in his parents' house, Simon dreamt of the adventures that awaited him now that his sight was uninhibited and his true priorities were determined.

Alone several years ago on his 15th birthday, Simon's spirit had broken. He had lost all hope- for himself, for society… for happiness, for contentment. Through the hopelessness that he felt, the true freedom that he now lived with was awakened, and it had all been leading up to this night. Losing all hope, stripping down his needs, and finding peace in pain had made him free, and he wouldn't trade it for the world.

The next few days saw Simon existing as if on auto-pilot, still completely preoccupied with the seemingly fictional occurrence of the recent evening. He would almost continually look at his hands, expecting them to be different, or at least bare some trace of the horror they had recently enacted. They looked the same… as did his face, eyes, and body. It was difficult to comprehend that something able to create such a mental metamorphosis in him had left barely a single physical trace. Short of a small bruise on his left forearm, which could have come from almost anything, he was unscathed.

The feeling of cautious empowerment had been in him long enough that it began to feel comfortable. It wasn't a happy feeling, nor one of contentment, but it was solid and clarifying. He had been in a nearly life-threatening situation and had maintained his composure, executed a plan, and killed a bully and a criminal that had probably been asking for it for decades; Not a pang of guilt or shred of remorse shared the space with the other emotions.

Simon was responsible for turning in a bit of homework, but was not expected to check in physically at school for a few more days. The profound differences in educational philosophies that he had experienced in his young life were astounding: The harsh confinement of boarding school *(which had been an exercise in futility for him)* and now the independent thinking, true learning oriented Open Door Academy, into which he was accepted due to exceptional test scores and a proven aptitude for success with self-study. He respected the current institution, the principles behind it, and even several of the educators. Their hands-off attitude evoked a sense of trust, and gave him confidence that he was not being written off as just another bundle of tax dollars. He felt invested in, and given his own chance to fail or succeed with a caring group of watchers to fall back on if struggles arose. It made him want to work, and strive to do well… neither of which any other learning environment had even come close to doing.

Simon spent a good part of his free time at the local mall. There was no better place to watch, listen, and learn about the widest cross-section of people and society, all without drawing a bit of attention to himself. He would walk, and sit, and occasionally buy a small drink or snack and talk to the cashier if they were open to it; He could tell as soon as he looked in their eyes whether it was worth attempting. Most were dormant, mindless robots barking preprogrammed phrases and not putting the slightest bit of critical thought into what they were doing or their surroundings. On a rare occasion Simon would find one so deplorable that once they delivered his order and went back into outer-space he would knock over the drink he had just purchased, usually onto the counter or somewhere near, just to witness some sort of emotion and draw forth an unscripted reaction.

Lately as he walked he had run across the same girl several times. Obviously not unusual to see people walking through a village, the difference here was the specificity with which she appeared to be traveling. Most people wandered, looking semi-lost, lackadaisical, and in no real hurry. She looked… pointed.

Not necessarily hurrying, but also beyond any doubt on some sort of mission. He had noticed her several times- the first unintentionally, and the next several less so. He was curious, which in and of itself was unusual. There were not five people on earth that Simon truly gave a shit about, and he liked that just fine.

She had taken the bus to the mall that day. He had ran, and walked, and by his estimation it took him about 20 minutes longer than she. Once there his goal was unspecific. He wanted to watch, and finding her would be fortuitous, but unlikely. The mall was disgusting. It boasted *"200 stores, 60 eateries!"* and unless there was a hidden section far beneath the ground that he had never seen, every single one was a useless drain on societies resources and a waste of the earth's valuable space. He would walk and sit as he usually did, and if his path crossed hers, so be it; it wasn't as if she would know either way.

The day found an unusual amount of kids in the mall. Kids in a mall is non-surprise, however today it was like an ant farm. He learned later that a school job fair had actually brought their students to the mall to *"investigate their options"*. No reason to set the bar high for the students... or for the country's future. Many of the suburban students at the mall were acting like uncaged animals... play fighting, following girls as if they were hunting in a pack in the wild, and running in and out of stores. It was almost too much to deal with... Simon was hoping for a nice quiet day of sociology, not a visit to a human zoo. His visit might be short. He kept thinking that the damned aren't even going to have to travel to hell... they're already there.

Seated half a mall block ahead of him appeared to be his unknowing muse... possibly an inaccurate term, but only in the sense that it suggested something was burgeoning. She had caught his interest and he wanted more; in that sense, it was true. He recognized the sweatshirt, and the posture. Having only once seen her in the daylight it would take a closer look to be sure, but judging by the way she was pretending to read the magazine she was holding and subtly watching a group of friends out of the corner of her eye, he was quite sure he had found his mark. He would not speak to her, nor would he look at her directly. He would walk by as a random stranger, spend 10 minutes watching her from afar, and walk back up the other side. She did not look like she was going anywhere. He wondered how long she had walked and perused to settle on that location, and if there were any other factors in play. There were a bunch of high school students in the area and... A dress and suit store. There was a dance approaching, they were preparing, and she wanted to watch. He immediately liked her even more.

Not a moment after the warm curiosity distracted him did he heard a commotion in the very direction he was headed. Not 15 feet from where she was perched, several bigger boys began picking on a smaller one. The smaller one was the proverbial runt- his clothes, posture, and response to antagonism told Simon that this was not the first time he had been tormented, and would not be the last. It looked harmless enough, and then the bigger boy pushed the prey into a small alcove, moved close to him, and struck his face. The boy was about to be beaten up with no potential recourse. One-on-one could be ignored, but more than that- he had a very personal sympathy for the small boy's situation, and chose to intervene. He had his blackjack, and a knife. Stabbing the boy would be too messy, too traceable, and too severe. Simon was a dead shot with his blackjack, even at a run, and knew he could knock the boy down and keep moving. He switched it from his inside coat pocket to his right hand, took a deep breath, and moved. He was a strong runner, having done it as often and as aggressively as he could his entire life, and the last several years had found him learning to incorporate other movements into his gait.

He came up on the boys, got a clean, brutal shot to the back of the largest's head, and kept going. He didn't look- he didn't need to. His forearm hurt from the blow, and even when practicing on trees and buildings, he seldom got that feeling. The boy was down, for sure, and the smaller one was free. He ran from the mall, and got almost halfway home before he became so winded that he had to stop.

CHAPTER IX.

Sarah had driven 217 miles between the moment she woke from a nap on Saturday afternoon and Sunday night when she called it quits for dinner and to prepare for the week. Mostly exploratory, she had performed only brief moments of true investigation. Driving on her own was far more compelling than she thought it would be and time had very much gotten away from her on both days. Her punishment of the week before was behind her now, and she would return Monday fully recovered from her brief illness, should anyone ask. Still a mystery was the fallout from the disruption last Tuesday. The day after had been quite a sight, as she imagined the rest of the week was, but she guessed that things would have quieted by Monday.

She could not have been more wrong. When Sarah arrived at Dyersville High on Monday morning it was as if there were a funeral in session in the Auditorium and Andrew had been a close personal friend of each and every student. A group of more morose, bleak-looking individuals she had never imagined… especially in this quantity. Littered throughout the school were flyers urging students to attend support groups with names like *"Comfort Hall" (an un-witty parody of the study hall period)* and her favorite *"The Cares and Prayers Group"* which was specifically for religious students that were having trouble dealing with the unsightly event and its possible, yet vague, parallels to biblical-type events. She was approached several times by faculty and guidance counselors who knew that she shared Journalism 8 with Andrew and asked if she needed to talk. Boy did she, but it was not about the pain and sadness she was feeling. How could an entire school be thrown off its' axis by the death of a student that was condescending to some, obnoxious to others, and acted like he was better than most? There was so much about common humanity that Sarah did not understand, and did not want to.

The day was awful. Nothing happened… classes were sparsely attended and unfocused, everyone was staring at their shoes and brooding, and Mahoney was absent from journalism. She could not wait to walk home in the cold. At least she would be alone, as opposed to being surrounded by sheep that were stuck mourning a lost soul that couldn't have cared less about them. Death was not always sad, and did not always warrant grieving … sometimes it was necessary, and important. Sometimes it evened life's imbalanced playing field… And sometimes it was just fate intervening where either learning, or genetics, or common decency had failed. No sooner would she feel badly for Andrew's demise than she would mourn the death of a drunk driver, or that of a robber who entered the *wrong* house. Interpersonal morality was not subjective… some things were good and some things were bad, and treating people like dirt, cheating, lying, and snobbery were despicable traits. Good riddance.

The weather was as bleak as the mood of the day. Light rain showers accompanied the wind and cold weather, and if Sarah wasn't so heated by her aversion to the behavior she witnessed today, she might have been uncomfortable. She walked with an uncustomary quickness, and was preoccupied wondering how she was going to relax enough to get to sleep tonight. Maybe she would go to the mall and read magazines- she did not have to be back with the car until 9pm, and even if her mother was as late as possible from work, she would still be home by 6:30pm. She would go home, eat, read a little, and go out. What perfect timing for her new freedom- without some sort of innocuous distraction, she would surely lay awake all night. The mall almost always served perfectly in that capacity.

Her mother arrived home at the usual time. Her father had been there for about 45 minutes, arriving just a half hour after Sarah at about 4:45pm. They both had pensive looks on their faces, and met her together at the door to her room. Her first thought was that some obscure relative had died. Her next thought was that something had happened to the car on her weekend journeys. Even her vivid imagination wouldn't have landed her on the truth; Mahoney had called her parents, concerned over Sarah's well-being due to her turbulent relationship with Andrew. He was worried that she was repressing feelings of guilt about the plagiarism situation of the month past and that she was not the sort to seek out counseling; He *was* right about that. She was immediately shut off… she did not want to discuss this with her parents and felt very hurt that Mahoney would reach out to her parents without talking to her first. None of this explained the true reason her parents were at her door.

"Sarah, I know you are probably upset that we spoke with your teacher.

We did not speak for you, nor did we give him any indication that we were worried about you. We know how mature and well- adjusted you are and although you do not communicate with us very much we would like to feel, and certainly hope, that if you were struggling with the things he mentioned that you would come to us." Her dad had spoken first, and she was relieved to hear that they had stayed on her side. Her mother chimed in. *"The issue we need to talk to you about is the plagiarism that* your father *discovered."* Sarah was speechless. Her mind had been too scattered today for her to have seen this coming, and she was dead to rights. *"Honey, we understand how hard it is to make friends in school… especially when you aren't the same type of social butterfly that many are… and making a discovery like that- well, we can understand how it would alienate you from your classmates and possibly even your teacher. We just don't know why you didn't tell us."* Her mother wasn't mad, just hurt. She felt that her daughter was in trouble and that she wasn't there for her. Sarah did not know how, but it appeared that this situation could turn in her favor.

"It just seems awfully elaborate. The way Mr. Mahoney described it I had read the story in the paper, gone in and found the matching issue, we had talked about it, and you had decided to bring it forward. That is quite a developed scenario. Should we be worried that you concocted that?" Her dad seemed much more ill at ease than her mother. She believed firmly and had thought often that to be where her mother was in her career she must have had to twist the chords of truth more than once. Her modest reaction to this situation was a relieving confirmation of that.

"Dad, I am so sorry. I didn't mean to discover that he had stolen the story… I was just going about my business and it came to my attention. I like Mr. Mahoney so much, and my journalism class, and I didn't want to see anything bad happen to him or to it. I wanted so much to ignore it all, but I couldn't. I suppose I did think quite a bit about the story- I

couldn't bear to just tattletale to a teacher I respect. I am so sorry I involved you, and I hope Mr. Mahoney can trust me again." Her dad nodded knowingly and gave a caring smile. *"Dear, we didn't tell Mr. Mahoney that your father did not discover the stolen story. As soon as he mentioned it, your father put him on hold briefly; we talked, and decided to keep it to ourselves. We know how hard high school is, and we don't feel we can do very much to help you. Maybe this will help a little."*

Sarah was so shocked and relieved that it felt like she was melting. Her arms felt longer, and it was hard to keep her eyes open. Her parents had saved her. She didn't know how she was going to next face Mahoney with him knowing she lied, and now she didn't have to. It could have done the exact opposite, but Mahoney's call today had instead brought her closer to her parents than anything else in young life had. She thanked them with a solemn look of appreciation and remorse on her face, and they smiled at her arm-in-arm as she walked back into her room. So much for the mall... the relief she was feeling right now washed any baggage she had kept from the day right out to sea. She could have fallen asleep standing up with her backpack on at that moment. After performing the favor of all favors for her tonight, the last thing she was going to do was ask her parents to borrow the car. After the talk they just had something common like that would seem to ruin the tone it had set.

Sarah rested as easy as she had in months despite the unsettling day. Truth had been her enemy today, but somehow she had managed to win the battle without even having to fight. Her mother had impressed her yet again, and she actually entertained in her semi-lucid state telling her mother about her exploits. As sleep came the notion was washed away- The line between acceptance of minor teenage indiscretions, and being receptive to the systematic elimination of people that had infringed upon Sarah's right to live unobstructed, was a very clear one and not to be crossed. Up to this point she had made no record or documentation of methods, details, mindset, or execution of any of her plans. She had always yearned to keep a journal of such things, but in truth, it would be the biggest liability of her life should she ever be discovered. Any potential of leniency, not guilty pleas, or simply not enough proof to link her to any of her acts would be out the window immediately should any trophy or paper trail come to light. She opted to keep everything stored in her mental journal, with the only physical documentation being vague and coded notes in a small paper tablet in the secret pocket of her backpack.

Sarah had been waking to thoughts of the religious implications of the burning. The sacrifices, purging... not things she usually entertained or even cared to acknowledge, but after witnessing the weight that the incident had put upon all visible attendees at Dyersville High, it began to enter her subconscious. She had previously dreamed of lakes of fire, of the burning of the immoral. The difference now was that it had lost any sense of generality. It immediately turned into Andrew Mahoney and the imagery placed him, in his burning form, into situations that had existed previously in her dreams. She jerked awake to the thought of Andrew at the base of her spiral staircase, screaming and writhing as the flames that melted him engulfed and turned to cinders the base of the endless ladder. She was perspiring with clenched fists when she woke, and both were very new to her. Sleep had always been a respite no matter the other turmoil- physical or mental- that was present in her life or in her mind. The idea of not being able to count on it was an entirely separate issue that was too troublesome to grasp. Right now she needed to understand and reckon what was left undone regarding the situation with Andrew, and close it. Something was keeping him alive in her mind, and today would be a day of pondering what that might be, and how she could eliminate it.

II.

Waking up late was not unusual for Simon. He was much more nocturnal than a bright, early morning person both due to his interests and pastimes, and the lack of a need to be anywhere specific before 11am but once a week. The events of the past days catching up with him had caused an unusual hibernation, but he woke feeling refreshed and back to full strength. His extended run was probably a bit much, and his legs and hips felt sore and warm, but strong. After a quick breakfast of scrambled eggs and chickpeas, he was off to school. The Open Door Academy was the antithesis of the Wolcott-North Academy where he had unintentionally spent most of his youth. As he arrived and entered the front door with his hood on, he was greeted pleasantly and by name by the security guard whom he was always cordial with. The man's name was Charles- a 40-something Hispanic man that appeared to have been through his own troubles, though Simon had never asked specifically. The tattoos on his neck and hands, even through the fading that time and hard living had caused, appeared to either be gang related or applied in prison. He was one of the most interesting features of the school; the number of incidents of student-related violence had almost disappeared since he came to work there over a year ago, as had the incidents of external graffiti on the building. He was always giving Simon the same knowing nod. *What did he know?* It was likely nothing more than a friendly understanding that Simon fell into the same outcast-type category that he did... but it was hard to believe that someone with the dark intuitiveness that kept him alive in whatever tumultuous situation he had grown up in didn't know something he wasn't saying out loud.

Simon often walked through neighborhoods that he could envision Charles living in, and he would think during his walks that if that were the case, it may be one of the reasons he stayed safe. He had not had more than a few conversations with Charles, and none were notable, however he was a figure that was on Simon's mind regularly. He was a mystery- an unlikely soldier of good fortune for the quirky private school, and an entirely different type of person than the rest of the faculty and staff. *Notably* so. The teachers and administrators at Open Door were all very good, and very appropriate for the M.O. of the school; all very learned, *"high-society"*, yet very figurative when it came to understanding many of the challenges the students faced and dealt with. They were soft, with very few exceptions, and Simon had made a science out of determining such things. In his prior school there had been several teachers that were obviously products of hard living, and a hard upbringing, and they bore physical and emotional marks that painted the picture. On the contrary here, most were mice, not even confident enough to keep eye contact for longer than a second, and Simon could make them physically uncomfortable with his very presence if and when he tried. Charles was the opposite. There was not one specific reason on earth that he should be so, however Simon was afraid of Charles. It was a feeling that for some reason made him feel very safe.

Today was assignment turn-in day. Once a week students are required to check in, attend a brief synopsis class for each of the subjects they are studying, and hand in assignments. Simon was religious about his homework. Many a night he would wander home at some ungodly hour after getting into who knows what kind of trouble, and would still have the presence of mind to complete an unfinished assignment. That attitude stemmed from an appreciation of the one place on earth where he felt *accepted*, and not even the slightest bit out of place. The least he could do was not make anyone's life there more difficult. He was quite an unlikely academic role model, but his grades were consistently exceptional. Setting the bar high for himself gave him something positive to focus on in the midst of the usually terrifying mental dialogue that ran in circles through his brain.

Of course, like any school, there were those that lived their lives to be insubordinate, and were amused to no end by misbehavior and insolence. Simon often glared at them, and succeeded occasionally in brow-beating them into silence. The general type that attended Open Door were hard workers that just followed the beat of a different drummer, however there were also a group that attended because they had either failed out of or been kicked out of public schools, and their parents had the money and clout to put them anywhere they wanted. It was obvious that the faculty had a distaste for them; possibly not obvious to all, but certainly to Simon. The polarization was blatant, and the groups did not really even intermingle. Simon mingled with no group, but was friendly with the *"good"* students, and was intentionally coarse and disturbing to the others. One of the only other reasons Simon could imagine that Charles acknowledged him or gave him the nod was that Charles was too an observer… and had likely seen Simon exert silent authority over misbehaver's. It was not a talent that could be taught, the ability to make people uncomfortable in complete silence. There needed to be intensity inside a person that it was possible to radiate out, thus disturbing the peace of the intended subject. He realized quite young that he could do this, and looked at it as an asset only to be used when necessary. Overuse, he felt, would dull the effect and also cheapen the process.

Simon felt it would have been better for his sanity and safety if he were required to be at school each day, however the actualization of it was much different. Of course there were classes available, but he was so much more in tune with the learning process when there were not interpersonal distractions to contend with. Imminently he would be focusing on another student's actions in class, or a certain manner of dress or conduct that puzzled, angered, or even occasionally intrigued him. At home he could immerse himself in what he was doing. His version of true learning required it... each piece of knowledge placed into a growing tool box that helped him live life by the codes and dictates he had set for himself. Even when a personal interest was not found in the material, as long as it may prove useful for even an unknown time in the future, he was never reluctant to put in the work needed to absorb the information. He didn't know how other students learned in a captive environment; he had somehow succeeded at it in his youth, however his ability to flip that switch and stay a productive part of any given group setting was long gone. Wolcott had chopped it down, and then poured on some gasoline to ensure it would not grow back.

Ending up at Wolcott-North Academy was in and of itself one of possibly two defining moments of Simon's early life. His parents were both from working-class families in a small UK town three hours east of London called Tyne and Wear. The setting offered few prospects for success growing up; it was largely a dock and shipping town- not surprisingly for most men, the options were working the docks, or working in shipping. Simon's father was a bright, resourceful sort and after a few years out of high school working as a longshoreman, had saved enough money and made enough local contacts to begin his own small shipping operation. He challenged the norm by incorporating an aggressive air freight network in a sea city, and when one of his high school chums found his way back home after a successful stint as a salesman in London, they teamed up and their small operation took off. Within five years it had been purchased with all its assets by the Norfolk Associates- the largest shipping conglomerate in Tyne. His father was guaranteed a salary for life and decided to take his newfound wealth, his new wife and young son, and move to America. It was truly one of the only rags-to-riches stories to ever come out of the small town and when he returns *(as they have once each year of Simon's life)* his father, Phillip Ravenhall, is treated like veritable royalty.

Life in America had held mixed results for his parents. It had been determined shortly after having Simon that his mother would be unable to bear any more children due to some complications that had arisen during the delivery. His father had remained bitter about it, stating all too regularly that if they had lived in America when Simon was born that the medical situation would not have occurred. Although the small UK town had bestowed upon him relative wealth and a moderate level of prestige, he held many grudges towards it for personal matters.

Simon and his father were not close.

As soon as he was old enough for the cognitive process to

truly activate, he began to feel as if his father was hoping-wishing even- for another chance when it came to offspring and was in a way disappointed that Simon was the only bearer of his lineage. As a boy Simon proved sharp- never overly athletic, competitive, or aggressive, but a quick study of sports and academics. He truly did not know what his father wanted, and without knowing, he felt it a waste and a risk to try to be anything that he was not.

His mother was nurturing, clearly loved her son, and had great sympathy for his plight. The only notion stronger than that, however, was her desire to not lose her husband. At this point, 19 years since the relationship had started, beginning again would be unfathomable. She had no marketable skills- she had worked briefly out of high school as a waitress, and subsequently as a paper-pusher at a shipping company. After that she held a token position at her new beau's upstart, and soon after, had never had to work again.

They traveled, and played, and it seemed to Simon that they were trying to reset the clock to a time before he was born and live their lives carefree from that point. *That* is how he ended up at Wolcott. It was a prestigious private school, and expensive, and as they called it, *all-inclusive*. This essentially meant that Simon's parents did not have to do *anything* for, with, or considering Simon unless they were so inclined. Holidays, birthdays, graduations, illness- all were handled by the school, and with the almost overwhelming ratio of faculty to students, there was always someone to play parent when something relevant was happening. Simon never warmed up to any of his faux family, and so the alienation and abandonment that he felt from day one in the 4th grade had manifested by grade 10 *(when he was granted transfer to Open Door)* into the controlled, calculated, and near-complete mania that was now his personality. It was not for the lack of others trying- there were many at Wolcott that had made themselves very available to Simon, but no matter how hard he tried, he could not see it as anything but disingenuous, forced courtesy and sympathy. Was the sympathy deserved? Possibly. But it was not wanted or accepted, much to the chagrin of the faculty and administrators at his little involuntary home away from home.

Simon was confident that his parents were kept up to speed on his unconventional behavior and his lack of interest in falling in line at the academy. He had begun to develop an animosity towards them as well- more so than what he harbored towards any of the faculty. Although leaving him to live their lives of denial was a tough pill to swallow, he could at least put his head around it. But when he had tried his best and was sinking beneath his own weight, not even contacting him to offer a word of encouragement was inexcusable, and devastating. It took some time, but the idea had occurred to him that if he behaved, he could use their absence and also their financial well-being to his advantage. Getting out became his goal, and all his actions and efforts began to center around it. Most students were doomed to complete their entire school career at Wolcott-North, and condemned to suffer long into their adult lives the repercussions of the social dwarfing that happened there. He wasn't going to have it, and the only out was to become exceptional. Proving that he had over-developed and outgrown the limitations of the academy was the only way to be transferred, and it was not without precedent. Several students each year were given *"Transfer Blessing"*, as it was pretentiously called, and were permitted to move into other structured, private learning environments. Simon did not care where, he did not care how. All he knew is that he wanted out, and no wall seemed too large to scale in order to reach that goal.

Almost as if twisting a faucet, Simon turned his personal interests, feelings, and inclinations off completely and began the process of assimilation he knew it would require in order to be deemed transfer-ready. In order to not seem contrived, Simon still kept to himself, but became a much more integral part of class settings and would even routinely ask teachers intelligent questions privately after class. He would spend the entirety of many classes fixed on one aspect of the topic at hand and formulating the question he would ask after class had ended. The hatred he developed for the other children of privilege that surrounded him was hard to contain, but it also strangely fueled his mission to escape. Never again did he want to feel like an outcast... even if he was. He now knew, even at the tender age of 14, that he must surround himself with people that shared his idiosyncrasies or no one at all. The idea of being alone, left to his studies and newly-developing interests in exploration and sightseeing, was almost too glorious to be a real possibility. He would pass hours of his off time just sitting on his bed thinking of the journeys he would undertake if he were free. The amount of time he spent alone garnered him a reputation as a freak, or some sort of weirdo. Wolcott was a very team-oriented group of students for the most part, and even with Simon's new integration into class settings, he still could not stomach the social side of the process. Several groups of the more athletic students (those of the *highest* privilege) made their dislike for Simon quite obvious and he knew that it would eventually come to a head. His choices were either to be ready, defend himself, and likely injure someone and be condemned to Wolcott forever, or take whatever they dished out and use it as leverage towards his exit plan. The choice was obvious to him, and the rationale was that no physical pain could match the turmoil that his current existence caused his brain every fucking day.

Mandatory physical education classes showed that Simon had a fair level of athletic prowess, and so his refusal to join *(or "contribute to" as it was called)* any structured sports teams was also frowned upon by his ultra-competitive peers. He could see in their eyes, as they had learned from generations of their pathetic parents passing the buck of personal responsibility, that every loss was at least partially blamed on Simon. Even though they had no proof to this end, he could *possibly* have tipped the scales in Wolcott's favor had he accepted the role of team player. It was truly pathetic, but the tension was building, and the most important thing is that he was aware of it.

His sharply turned academic performance was also alienating. There was a strange hierarchy within the school, and the dominant athletic performers were also expected to be the academic leaders. In a rare showing of balanced education, WN made sure that the students did not leave apt in one thing and lacking in another, clinically speaking. Behaviorally was an entirely different issue.

As Simon continued to excel in his studies and sow the seeds of his exit strategy, he became a little bit more polarizing each day. He was becoming something of a pariah, although it was still subtle enough that the administration did not feel the need to intervene. They did not deal well with student conflicts or social outcasting; the concern was both from a liability perspective and was also complicated by the *"all are equal under the Wolcott banner"* rhetoric that was sickeningly present in all literature and in each and every group seminar or pep rally. It was in truth such a farcical notion that it made Simon sick whenever he heard or thought of it. The only way he could be more of an outcast was if he happened to be Asian or African-American. There were only one or two of each in the entire school, and watching how they were treated was deplorable. Simon was not a champion of any cause but his own, however watching the hypocritical operation of the Academy on a daily basis drove him to near-madness, and he wanted to unearth it all; expose them for what they really are- small-minded elitists breeding more of themselves and weeding out those that won't *"make the cut"*. He wanted to execute them all by firing squad, making them look their executioner in the face prior to their termination. Or better yet, make them beg in front of each other and then when the time came, fire blanks. Their fragile high-society egos would be forever broken, and they would wish they had, in fact, died.

III.

The eggshells that Simon had been walking on amongst his peers had finally begun to crack within view of the administrators. Several members of the faculty had approached him and requested a *"consult"*, which was the term they used for a not-mandatory-but-recommended conference regarding behavior, academic shortcoming, etc. Since his academic performance was stellar, he knew the request was in regards to his lack of integration into the Wolcott-North lifestyle. He had put off their request for weeks, and dared not do so any longer for fear of it impacting his goals. He accepted, and during his free period at 2pm he was scheduled to see Mr. Lisi, an older member of the faculty that pulled double duty as counselor and Coach of the football and lacrosse teams.

"Simon Ravenhall... how are you son?" Lisi seemed to be a straight shooter, and Simon was going to have to be crafty to outwit him on home turf. *"I am doing well sir. Trying to stay focused on studies this term. I know my tendency to get distracted, and so I'm paying extra attention to doing well."* *"You certainly are. Your parents must be very proud of your grades. You're in the top 1% of your class right now, with no signs of slowing down. Very good. With all the distractions at your age it is commendable for a young person to excel at learning."* Simon had a solid guess where they were going next, and played along. Smiling shyly, he offered his thanks. *"Mr. Lisi, it is difficult here for me, but I want to do well. Do you have any advice for me going forward?"* Lisi smiled, and it was obvious after all these years his ego still enjoyed a nice stroking. *"Son, we only have a half hour... advice going forward would take a month! If I had to recommend one thing for someone of your discipline and good behavior it would be to not forget to be a boy- get out there and play on the sports teams- make some friends in some clubs or activities. Your standardized physical tests are quite good- I know you won't have any problem finding a spot somewhere that interests you."*

Simon put his head down, and crafted his response. *"Sir, I feel strongly that if I spread myself too thin I won't be able to concentrate the energy needed on my studies. I want my parents to see my high grades- they aren't going to come visit, so them watching me play sports isn't motivating to me. They'll see my grade reports, and that is the only way I can show them that I'm doing well here."* Lisi looked confused, and even slightly frustrated. *"We build well-rounded individuals here Simon- grades alone will not allow you to take in the real Wolcott experience. We would like you to try to take steps to be less reclusive. We need you to explore your other interests besides studies and think about providing yourself a more well-rounded educational experience. Does that make sense?"* Simon was still stuck on Lisi's instruction to *"explore his other interests"*, but had to snap out of it quickly and exit the

conversation. *"I understand sir. My interests right now lie in proving myself to my parents, and excelling in my studies, but I will look around and determine what else it would benefit me to spend time pursuing."*
"I'm glad we were able to spend this time Simon. You are a bright prospect here, and I hope you will reach your potential." Lisi's final tone was almost dark, and there was the faintest hint of intended intimidation in his voice. Simon was not intimidated, but did feel that he would soon be on a radar he did not want to be on if something did not change.

The process of self-evaluation was not one he was opposed to, however he did not have any interest or intention of using it for the purpose Lisi suggested. Quite the contrary; his evaluation would entail determining how to use the hostility of his peers towards his end of getting a stamp of approval to leave. He had no intention of integrating into any clubs or sports teams. No matter how hard he tried, or how much he pretended, there was no way Simon could appear convincing in a role that involved team play and competitive spirit. He wanted Wolcott to lose. He wanted the athletes to get injured, and to suffer horrible, embarrassing defeats. If anything, he would wish as hard as he could for their misfortune, and then go and watch in hopes that it would manifest. Fuck Lisi, Simon thought. That smug prick didn't care about him any more than he cared about any non-athletic standout. His job and motivation were one- and it was to groom the next season of sports sheep to ensure Wolcott's continued success in the Class B team standings. Simon's well-being was not a care of Lisi's… especially after the inconclusive consult they had, and his unwillingness to jump with both feet into the *"Wolcott experience"*.

It had been a week since the meeting with Lisi, and the facade of quiet, clean-cut "*A*" student that Simon had manufactured was taking on water. His isolation and reluctance to attend even the most innocuous of social functions was beginning to draw attention to him. Several of the top athletes in the school had already taken to giving him the stare- a tough look that Simon guessed was supposed to tell him non-verbally that he was in danger, or that he was disliked. Simon chose to keep those types of feelings to himself. Inconspicuous dislike or want for harm is much more dangerous than any overt, childish stare-down or taunting. Also obvious was the extent to which Simon's lack of reaction bothered the boys. He remained neutral while in receipt of hostility, and that too fueled the fire. Something was coming, and it wasn't far off. He was shoved from behind today and did not even turn around to unveil his assailant. He did not care, and nothing they could do will make him care. They are temporary ticks on his hide- no more than an annoyance that will come back into his mind when he's older as an example of why he needed to take the path he took. The path of solitude he had chosen will have its' roadblocks, but none will be disruptive enough to derail him. Achieving true independence was his destiny, set in motion by his intense awareness at an early age, and given legs through his long-developed distaste for society and all but the rarest of people he came in contact with.

Solid sleep had been eluding Simon for several nights, this being no exception. The slightest noise would bring him awake with a start, and even the white noise of the furnace would break his slumber. He was growing more and more unsettled, and sleep was the first casualty. Tonight he had heard laughing, which meant nothing more than a few students sneaking somewhere after curfew. Not a rarity, and since it sounded like it came from at least one floor down, it was thought nothing of. Simon had only momentarily faded back to sleep when his door opened and four boys piled in wearing handkerchiefs over their faces and talking in loud whispers. Finally, he thought briefly. *Here it is.*

Two boys grabbed Simon, assuming he would be doing his best to get away, and the others began hitting him with pillowcases filled with what felt like shoes, or baseballs. He imagined he would be unconscious soon, and it would all be out of his hands. The pain he felt in the meantime was nothing more than a rite of passage; a due he had to pay to earn the right to exist outside societies confines. *"You fuckin' freak…"* one whispered at him *"none of this would be happening if you just tried to be normal." "Everyone knows you think you're special… how special do you feel now freak?"* Simon remained silent, trying to look into the eyes of his attackers so he could identify them later. The pain was formidable, he could now feel blood running down his face, and he had a very warm, stinging sensation in his midsection. One of the boys hit him with his fist, and another kicked at him with booted foot. He was sure that several fingers were broken, and possibly his collarbone. He was facing sideways on the ground now, looking out the small crack under the door and wondering if anyone would come to his aid. Although not in full possession of his faculties, he was quite sure he saw the shadow of feet outside the door on the right. He was struck once more with the pillowcase in the back, given a sharp kick to the back of his head, and then as quickly as they had come the boys disappeared. Simon drifted off to sleep with no attempt to move, though he would have been incapable of doing so even if he had wanted to.

He awoke to two nurses' aides chattering about what to do

until the ambulance got there, and settling on nothing. They left him on the floor where he had been all night, and he could feel his head resting in a pool of warm liquid. The rest of his body was immobile and tingly, with the exception of his stomach, which stung and burned and felt moist. His hands would not open, and he had given up trying to roll to his back. He would stay quiet and wait now. Favor would be turning towards him soon.

He must have looked quite bad, because the ambulance crew came in looking dormant and immediately shifted into high gear upon first examination. Unsure of his injuries, they braced his head and lifted him gently onto a wheeled bed that took him to the vehicle. His stomach hurt badly now, and his entire body was throbbing and he felt like he might vomit. He took breaths as deep as he could to avoid doing so, and was given something as soon as he entered the ambulance that put him back to sleep. As he was drifting, he saw Lisi standing outside the back doors. While flashing back to their meeting, he fell into a chemical sleep that he did not wake from for almost two days.

IV.

Simon woke up in a hospital room, alone. He was very relieved when he could wiggle his toes, move his uncasted fingers, and see out of both eyes. He knew he wasn't paralyzed, and anything else he could recover from. He had been awake for about 10 minutes when a nurse came in and looked relieved to see him conscious. *"Well now, Simon, nice of you to join us."* She smiled, and he attempted to as well. His face hurt, and his head felt humongous. *"You have been asleep since Monday, and it is now Wednesday afternoon. You should be better rested than anyone in this hospital!"* He appreciated her attempts at humor, and at lightening the mood. She was pretty, probably in her 40's, and obviously a true soul. She was not one that did it just for the money; the look of relief on her face when she saw his eyes was not something she could fake. He was glad that his temporary caretaker was genuine, and sorry that he had worried her. *"I'll tell the doctor that you're up, and he will be in to see you soon. You really need to get some new friends... or stop stealing people's lunch money. You are lucky this wasn't any worse, and I'm very glad it wasn't as well."* Smiling again, she left at a brisk pace, undoubtedly going directly to the doctor. He wanted to see himself. She was acting slightly uncomfortable, and for someone that has likely seen the horrors and dealt with the mortality that she has, it made him curious as to his condition. He would know soon he imagined, but for now, he would rest. Closing his eyes felt extraordinary. Nothing so simple had ever given him so much pleasure, and it was not something he would soon forget.

He awoke to the voice of a male doctor talking to the nurse from before. They were discussing his pain medication regimen and their attention shifted to him as soon as he opened his eyes.

"Simon, I'm Dr. Wells. I'll be taking care of you for the rest of your stay here. As Vanessa told you, we're lucky this was not any worse. I have some officers that have been waiting to speak with you as soon as you were able, would you mind if I sent them in after I check you out?" Simon was not nearly the fan of the doctor that he was of Nurse Vanessa. *"I'm not interested in talking to officers about what happened. Please tell them I don't know. I was awakened in the dark by the boys. By the time it was all over, my eyes still hadn't even adjusted. I couldn't be of the slightest help."* Simon had no intention of outing his

attackers to conventional authorities. True darkness did not exist at Wolcott; there was always the maddening glow of the outdoor lights, and they had allowed Simon to identify all but one of his attackers by physical characteristic, process of elimination, and their eyes. Ever since he had first felt hostility rising months ago, he had begun surveying the eyes of his potential assailants. It was plain as day who harbored the most ill will towards him, and he had paid them extra attention. Afterwards, he was confident that he could name 3 of them, and that was enough. He had known all along that the attack would happen, and although the aftermath was sure to be trying, as long as he was able to walk out of the hospital soon and of his own power, it was all worth it.

"Well Simon, I know the police will be very disappointed. They take things like this very seriously, and when something this severe occurs and a student has to be admitted into the hospital, they want to place blame. Please let me or Vanessa know if anything occurs to you and we will tell the officers." The doctor was not entirely lying... Wolcott took this type of thing *very* seriously when it seeped outside their doors. Whoever the ringleader was of Simon's attempted attitude adjustment was certainly catching hell right now for going overboard and making it something that the on-site nursing staff couldn't deal with, bandage up, and send away. Undoubtedly there would be negative attention garnered due to the attack; although he would not perpetuate it in any way, or encourage any investigation, he would now be on everyone's radar and must engineer it to his advantage.

"All that aside Simon, I want to update you on your condition. You have been semi-sedated for several days to allow some swelling to subside in your head. You have a concussion, and we thought you may have a slight skull fracture, however luckily you do not. As you can see, we casted your right

hand. You have three broken fingers and a sprain in your wrist that was serious enough that immobilization was best. You will likely need to have the cast on for 3-4 weeks, so no sports." No sports, the doctor had said. Humorous only in the sense that if he had walked cooperatively into the footprints laid out for him and been involved in them, he would likely not be in this situation.

The doctor continued *"You undoubtedly feel a pain in your stomach. One or several of the blows you received ruptured your spleen, and we needed to remove it upon your arrival here. You are lucky that someone found you when they did- that is a very serious injury if left untreated. You will see when you are able to make it to a mirror that we have placed stitches in several areas throughout your head and face, and you have two broken ribs."* Simon was now beginning to realize the gravity of the situation, and the pain he felt intensified as the doctor described the various injuries.

"You will be in this bed for another few days, and probably in hospital care for a week or so. One of these injuries on their own wouldn't warrant such measures, but it is a volatile combination, and we intend to err on the side of caution. Hopefully later tomorrow we will move you in to bathe and the following day Vanessa will shuttle you around in a wheelchair. Simon, we have spoken with your parents, and although they will not be able to be here, they have arranged for you to have the best possible care, sparing no expense. Please let us know if you need anything." Seething, but unsurprised, Simon made his request. *"I would like a book. '1984' by George Orwell please."* The doctor smiled smugly. *"You sure you wouldn't prefer some magazines or a video game?"* *"I am beyond sure, Dr. Wells. Thank you."*

V.

There was an ever so slight squish as Sarah unintentionally

drove over the frog that had hopped into the street on her way to the mall. She was developing into quite a good driver, but still did not have the confidence to dart about to avoid small hazards. She had driven through several possibly avoidable potholes over the past weeks, and tonight the frog. She had seen it in the headlights and asked it silently not to hop in the road, but it had not heard. Instinct caused her to want to stop, but she knew it to be no use. She felt badly that something attempting to live its' life in peace had been destroyed at her hand, and as she often did, she began to wonder about the roots of those feelings. As it had been doing for weeks, her mind shifted to Andrew Mahoney, and she remained unsettled the rest of the drive. No amount of thinking had brought Sarah to any conclusion or epiphany regarding the lingering ghost of Andrew. The closest thing she could muster was that she had truly done something that was outside her current capacity, and coming to grips with it was taking time. It was certainly the most dramatic incident she had ever created, or witnessed, or possibly even heard about, and she may have been underestimating its emotional gravity. The other recurring theme of thought is that she was feeling this way because she had inadvertently harmed Mr. Mahoney- someone she cared for and wished to protect. He was affected greatly by the situation, and was without a doubt feeling guilt for the harsh words he had spoken about Andrew mere weeks before his brutal demise. He had not been the same in class since- distant, and morose- and Sarah needed to figure out what she could do to help without letting on *why*.

Relating to him in some way regarding their mutual mixed feelings towards Andrew was the most plausible scenario, but she would need to be very careful to maintain her neutrality towards him prior to the plagiarism incident. It must never be brought into question that her motive was anything but the sanctity of the school paper.

Sarah would remind herself during times like this that an advantage of not having friends was that there was no one to worry about having to mistrust. Her parents had proven beyond a doubt that they were on her team, and anyone else she was even remotely close to was an adult, and completely removed from her personal life. The closest thing she had to a friend was nothing more than a mysterious shadow that she had all but written off the chance of ever meeting face-to-face. She did consider Mahoney a friend of sorts, however her guard was all the way up when around him because she could sense his intuitiveness, and did not have any desire to challenge its aptitude.

The mall brought the very type of group solitude that Sarah was craving. Alone in a crowd, she wandered for over an hour, thinking of everything under the sun and only focusing her eyes on inanimate objects; she felt that if she were to look people in the eye in her current state of mind that they might see her for what she truly was, or even worse, start a conversation with her. She chose one corner of the mall to stand in even though it was an area that made her uncomfortable. Adjacent to the pet center and a small piercing pagoda there were some pay phones, a photo booth, and several benches. It seemed to be a place that everyone stopped at some point, and she liked the variety of scenery. She severely disliked the pet store. She did not desire a pet, but each time she saw its unsettled and grotesquely cramped inhabitants, she wanted to take *all* of them home.

Of course that was the intention, and she guessed that the

notion of impulse buy was the store's strongest allure. She could see at that moment three young children on the verge of a fit, tugging at their parents' coats with urgency, attempting to rescue the victim they had deemed most needy. The man working the counter looked like one of the underfed animals he kept hostage. He reminded her for some reason of a disingenuous mall Santa Claus- another figure that held the key to child's hearts and dreams, yet only succeeded to anyone paying attention in coming off like a soulless opportunist. Sarah was standing still, confused by her compassion towards the simplest of mammals and the complete lack of it towards the most complex, when she was approached by a familiar face.

"Sarah! Hi- I'm surprised to see you at the mall. You don't seem the type." It was Maria- the girl she had interviewed for her article in the paper. *"I mean, I guess everyone comes to the mall occasionally, but you seem to be hanging out here. It's cool."* Sarah smiled, and tried to shake the cobwebs from her head to enter into a conversation. *"Well, occasionally I like to come here and read magazines in the book store- do you guys do that?"* Maria was with another girl that only looked about 75% as unusual as she, and was much prettier. *"Oh yeah- Feldman's Booksellers has asked us to leave many times because they know we almost never buy anything. We read magazines, and I think they expect that, but one time we sat down in an aisle and looked at some books, and from then on they've been hard on us."* Sarah laughed like she cared. *"Hmmm, that's too bad. If I couldn't read in the mall, I wouldn't be here nearly as often! I'm not a big shopper."* Maria's eyes changed tone, and Sarah knew why before a word was spoken. *"Sarah, I haven't talked to you since Andrew died. I know you knew him from Journalism class. I'm sorry if you guys were friends."* *"Thank you Maria. We weren't close, but anyone you have a class with all year seems like a friend in a way, you know? It*

was a shocking situation, that's for sure."

After a pause, and looking at her friend, Maria spoke again. *"I saw you the... the day it happened. Down by the lunch room. Everyone else was panicking and you... well, you just looked like you look now. You must have been in shock."* Sarah wanted to deviate away from the topic immediately. Nothing she could say would help Maria understand why she stood emotionless watching a classmate burn to death, and it certainly wasn't worth trying. *"Maria, did you witness the event as well? How are you?"* Looking at her shoes, she answered *"I came over towards the end. I couldn't watch, so instead I watched the people in the halls. It was terrible. I felt so badly for everyone, including you. You must have felt so helpless, especially since you knew him. I'm not trying to bring up uncomfortable feelings for you, but my counselor told me that talking about this with people that shared the experience would help us all heal."* Sarah smiled warmly, *"Oh, it's OK Maria... I understand. Keeping it all to yourself is just too much to bear. It was nice to see you today. What is your friend's name?"* Maria answered quickly, and mortified, *"My god! The nerve of me- I'm sorry- this is Angela. She goes to Open Door Academy across town."* *"Nice to meet you Angela."* The girl smiled. She was pretty and also obviously harboring something, since she did not utter a word the entire time that Sarah and Maria talked, but her eyes did not leave either speaker for a moment. She was obviously a watcher. *"Maria, thank you for talking about Andrew."* Sarah mustered all the conviction she could *"It helped me to talk a little today."* Maria smiled through the black lipstick she was wearing. Her outfit was not nearly as bizarre as the initial one that Sarah remembered, but it was still not flattering in any way. Maria surely left feeling that they were friends, and that was certainly the intention- especially after the discovery that Maria had been watching her reaction during the burning. There were only a few moments during the situation that Sarah was not fully aware of her surroundings, and they must have coincided with moments of her observation. She was certainly engrossed for several minutes, staring into the flames as if they were the only thing in the world to be looked at.

Much to her surprise, she *did* feel better after talking about Andrew. Possibly even just trying to convince someone that she was feeling badly helped her feel a bit more normal about the situation. She felt briefly grateful to Maria, and next considered talking to her parents to see if it worked again. Did her version of closure include fabricating *"normal"* feelings about the situation and sharing them with those who cared? She was not above it, especially if it got her back to sleep and feeling herself.

Darkness had fallen while she was standing in the corridor, and that meant it was time for one more pass and then a drive home. Maria was an unexpected twist to her mall trip, that's for sure, but possibly one that opened her eyes to something important in finding closure. If she did not insist on looking so odd, Sarah may have considered her a friend. As she was, however, she would be an easy liability and stood out far too much to be kept in Sarah's company.

Upon arriving home, Sarah found her parents reading sections of the local paper in the living room, seated opposite each other and both looking quite sleepy. She put on a face that would let them know she had something worrisome on her mind, and walked into the room. With her best puppy-dog eyes and furrowed brow, she looked at the floor as if overtaken with emotion. They immediately picked up, and her mother spoke first.

"Sarah dear, what is it? You are obviously not OK." Sarah nodded

3 856007 103650

Croatia's unc

meekly and her father stood up, put his arm around her, and sat her down on the couch. She kept looking down and tried unsuccessfully to cry a little bit. With one of her parents on each side of her, she began. *"I don't think I gave myself enough time to deal with what happened to Andrew. The last few days I've been feeling really terrible and haven't been sure why, but I think I am still feeling guilt over what happened with the paper... and now that he's dead... I mean, I can't even imagine how he must have been feeling leading up to that. I feel like I might have made the last weeks of his life a little bit miserable, and I feel just awful."* Her parents looked at each other surprised, but also with relief. The unaffectedness that Sarah had projected after the incident had surely worried them, and this show of naked humanity had somewhat eased their minds.

"Dear, you are no more responsible for Andrew's happiness than your mother or I. He used bad judgment in stealing the story for the paper. That does not take away from the tragedy of his death, and it is unfortunate that the two things happened in such close proximity, but none of it falls on you. You did the right thing reporting the incident. Had you not done so and something happened as a result, you would undoubtedly feel much worse." Her mother had seen a more emotional side to it, which was a change in roles. *"Andrew did not deserve to die, but I can see how you feel badly knowing he did so still harboring feelings about the situation with the paper. Sarah, you just have to take comfort in knowing that Andrew knew he was wrong, and was probably just looking for forgiveness, not revenge. Anyone who steals anything knows they are wrong, and I'm sure he was still hurting, but I also know that he did not wish any ill will on anyone involved with the situation."*

Her parents were helpful, and much to her surprise, speaking openly about what she thought her feelings should be towards the situation helped her relax. It did seem, after all, that the appearance of normalcy was helping greatly in her *feeling* normal. She couldn't yet say for sure, but she was anticipating a good night's sleep. She had Maria to thank for it, and felt as if she now owed her some sort of nicety. Possibly she would meet her at the mall? She was also curious about Angela, and an added dimension was that she had often wondered *(based mostly on geography of her sightings)* if the boy she sought may also attend the Open Door Academy. She didn't know how Angela could help her determine such a thing, or even how she would approach it, but things like that came easy to her when the situation presented itself. Perhaps she would ask Maria to go to the mall the following weekend. She would take a few days to warm up to the idea, and then make a final decision on Thursday.

The early days of the week had come and gone, and the only thing not even keel was her parents' treatment of her since their talk. They were handling her as if she might break, more like a fragile item of curiosity than a durable, resourceful teenage girl. The coddling was nice for a minute, but by Wednesday it had become tiresome, and she did not want any more of it. She had treaded an unexplored path in talking about her emotions and feelings with her parents, and she may have overdone it. All she could do is ride it out and wait for them to see that she was OK, and not on the verge of some sort of adolescent made-for-TV breakdown. Already determined was that she would see Maria on Friday and ask if she was interested in a mall trip over the weekend. Sarah had been sleeping better; her nightmares were at least back to normal, and it was Maria who had cleared that path. The least Sarah could do is spend an afternoon with her to show her gratitude.

The fallout from the school tragedy was making national news with record numbers of student absences and the school's unprecedented toleration of it. Students were given extra *"personal days"* to help them deal with their feelings regarding the situation, and it all cleared with the school board and superintendent in light of the horrifying nature of the incident. It was quite a debacle. Classes were still not back to normal, and there was even some scuttlebutt about more than a few parents pulling their students and enrolling them in private school. The feeling of vulnerability was not subsiding, and with it came the reactionary crowd that waits in the wings for things of this nature to happen and then, well, reacts. There were new bills on school safety, new proposals on fire prevention for students, extinguisher placement… as if there was a coming epidemic of student spontaneous combustion.

A band aid only works if there is a visible wound to heal, and at least in Sarah's mind, all the healing left to be done was far deeper than the reach of the school board and their trivial procedural updates. No matter. She was on her own twisted path to recovery, and that is all she need be concerned with right now. The sheep that walked alongside her at Dyersville High were already lost; the situation with Andrew was merely another detour. It was a separating of the herd… the weak crumbled and did not recover, and the strong kept their composure and maintained their responsibilities, even in the face of discomfort. Life itself is uncomfortable by nature; assuming otherwise will only lead to heartache. Sarah felt it was best to expect the worst and be occasionally surprised by a positive outcome. Expecting things to go well will most often just lead to disappointment.

Maria was walking towards her, presumably on her way to lunch. Slightly nervous, Sarah flagged her down and smiled.

"Maria! How are you?" "I'm fine Sarah… I've had a tough week, I'm very glad it's almost over. How are you?" "Fine as well. Thanks for talking with me last week at the mall. I needed that." Maria looked surprised at the sentiment, but received it well. *"Oh, any time. I was nervous to talk to you, truthfully. I wasn't expecting you to be interested."* Sarah smiled modestly and looked at the ground. *"Well, I was planning a mall trip this weekend, and was wondering if you were interested in going. I'm just hoping to read some magazines, walk around, and watch the world go by. It's OK if you have plans already. Of course Angela is welcome as well."* Sarah could have slapped Maria right across the face and she may not have looked as surprised as she did at the offer of a mall trip. *"I would love to go to the mall. Thank you. I know Angela would also love to go. Shall we meet you there?" "Sure… but if you were having trouble finding a ride, I could pick you up. Take my number down? We could go any time in the afternoon."* Maria looked elated. They exchanged numbers, and with that, the first social plans of Sarah's high school career were made official.

CHAPTER X.

Consideration of personal appearance was something that Sarah minded each and every day, but not within the context of a social outing. She always wanted to appear neat, clean, and kept at school but now, with her mall plans approaching within the hour, she felt an unusual desire to dress for it. She opted for a long blue coat instead of her hooded sweatshirt, and matched her shoes to it. She fixed her hair, leaving it down but pulled back out of her face. She felt confident, and even through all the nervous anticipation was excited about the day.

Maria had called her and said that they had access to a car and would meet her at the mall in front of the pet store at 2:30pm. Sarah was partially hoping that they needed a ride; she was very curious as to where and how Maria lived and to discover more information about Angela. There was still an element of strangeness to the idea of such a conventionally pretty girl keeping such unconventional and troubled company. The idea of Angela potentially having information about the human figment of her imagination seen lurking in the woods was still present in her mind, but she held for it little hope. It may have been two different people, the interloper from the mall and the stranger with the lit cigarette. Sarah's romanticizing of it had begun to feel silly to her, and she was making efforts to cast it aside in lieu of healthier thoughts. The forming of a friendship with Maria was a start, and was intended more as therapy than enjoyment; her recent attempts at normalcy had done a great deal to quiet the raucous in her mind, and what was more normal than teenage girls meeting at the mall?

Always punctual and attentive, Sarah arrived in front of the pet store five minutes early and stood with her back to the corner as she often did while watching the human shopping carousel parade by. She would surely see Maria and Angela as soon as they came in, and it gave her a much needed sense of confidence to know that she would see them first. Performing her relaxing breathing, she waited and watched, and wondered if the step she had taken towards social integration would prove a good idea. 10 minutes had gone by and it was then that Maria, flanked by Angela, walked through the front doors of the mall. They walked right by Sarah, and she pretended not to notice in order to not seem over eager. Looking in the window of the pet store and keeping them in her sights in the reflection, she turned as she saw them turn, and they greeted happily. *"Hi Sarah! Sorry we're late, my 13 year old brother was bothering us and I couldn't keep him away… he kept hiding my shoes and asking us if we were going to the mall to meet boys. I think he has a little crush on Angela, and it is SOOOO annoying!"* Sarah smiled, and said she had only been there a minute herself. Angela smiled and greeted her quietly, her pale blue eyes glistening like gems, and appearing much larger than Sarah remembered. Angela was striking. She did her best to neutralize it, but her beauty and sadness radiated through in equal measure, and both in truly dramatic form. Sarah felt herself stare for a minute too long, and Angela looked away, uncomfortable. Maria had made an effort to look less menacing, and Sarah obeyed the compulsion to acknowledge it. *"Maria, I really like your shoes! I'm glad you were able to find them… and I didn't notice in school this week, but have you had a haircut?"* Maria beamed, and stammered briefly in her response. *"Oh… I have been saving these shoes for a special occasion, and it's kind of embarrassing but my mother used to be a hairdresser and has always cut my hair. Thank you for noticing."* The idea of siblings had been racing through Sarah's mind since Maria brought it up, and the very premise was too overwhelming for her to even comprehend. Someone living in your house that you were forced to love and care for even if all they did was annoy you and make your life miserable? She felt very grateful to her parents at that moment for choosing to allow her to develop without that permanent burden. Life, and certainly young adulthood, was difficult enough without that sort of aggravation.

The girls began their stroll through the mall just like so many before them. Sarah on the left, Maria in the middle, and Angela a half a step back and to the right. They would walk a lap or two and then settle in at the bookstore for a while. Less than halfway down the first corridor of their journey, a group of four boys shouted something derogatory at Angela as if they knew her. Maria came to her defense reflexively, as if it had happened before, and the boys laughed and continued the other way. They had said something about her pants, and the loony bin. Sarah wished she would have heard it in its entirety, but from the look on Angela's face, it hit home and was not something she wished to discuss. *"Most boys are such assholes"* Maria exclaimed, back to her normal demeanor. Seeing her turn into an attack dog so quickly showed that there was certainly another side to her… a side that did not surprise Sarah in the slightest. Someone who chose to look and behave like she did had undoubtedly taken plenty of abuse, and the fact that she had stayed so generally amicable and friendly in the face of it all was admirable. *"That same group of boys has shouted at us more than once… I just wish they'd leave us alone. Two of them go to Open Door with Angela, and the other two go to Dyersville with us, unfortunately. I see them wandering around the halls and sometimes just wish they'd trip and fall down some stairs!"* Maria laughed it off, and Sarah briefly pictured the engineering behind a *"trip"* down the stairs. Angela's expression had shifted back from traumatized to her usual one of morose. They had taken a lap and Sarah used the turning of a corner to move closer to Angela. *"I have always been curious about Open Door. Do you like it?"* Happy to be addressed, Angela smiled meekly and responded. *"It's school, after all, but it could be a lot worse. They really let you do everything at your own pace and you're basically just responsible for completing work… where you do it, or even when, is up to you. It either works for people or it doesn't. For me, it's great. I go to school for about a half a day, and then do all my work in my room, listening to music, or whatever."* Sarah was stunned at the very idea of a learning institution being trusting enough to let students go *anywhere* at their own pace or of their own free will. It seemed like a privilege reserved for adults, and very risky. Angela continued, *"They really emphasize people finding what they like to do… they know that everyone isn't cut from the same mold, and won't be good at the same things. It's nice. I hate math, and so I only have to take a little bit of it, and can use my notes for tests. I love to write and paint and I love learning about history, and so I focus on those subjects and keep good grades."* Sarah was open-mouthed at the progressiveness of the ideas that Angela was putting forth. She wanted to know more, but didn't want to seem a nosy inquisitor. *"That sound amazing Angela, I'm jealous! I hate Dyersville High except for my Journalism class. I would love to be able to focus on writing and skip science!"* She had complimented and related with Angela, and had gotten the same little smile she had received when they arrived at the mall. She felt as if with the voicing of her discontent, Angela had begun to accept her. She wanted to open the door wider, but thought it best to move slowly. The incident with the boys further confirmed that in some way Angela was damaged goods, and Sarah didn't want to scare her off.

They settled in the bookstore and read magazines, seated near each other but not interacting. It felt nice to be on her own, but also knowing that she had company to call on if something noteworthy occurred. She could fathom repeating the trip to the mall with her new friends. It was interesting to think that just an hour before she was to meet them, she considered calling it off because of how sure she was it would be a disaster. This was the occasional positive outcome that Sarah never expected, but welcomed. Angela stood first, and wanted to walk some more. Maria was reading a magazine that featured women covered in tattoos, and looked quite frightening. Sarah had settled on *Outdoor Adventures*, mostly due to the cover boasting an entire section on the skinning and preparing of various hunted animals. There must be similarities to the species that Sarah hunted, and she would put what she could in her memory bank. Angela had chosen a book- *"Wicca and Witchcraft"* and the picture on the cover depicted a goat head inside a small circular symbol with some non-English writing surrounding it. It looked subversive, and interesting, and very much up Angela's alley. She bookmarked her place in it with a small piece of paper and put it back behind some other books on the shelf. The girls began to roam again and chatted all the while. It was nearing time to go, and it seemed as if none of them wanted to. Sarah was learning quickly that finding those you can relate to was uncommon for people like them, and made for an immediate bond.

Her first social outing had gone swimmingly, and she had plenty to think about prior to their next one. She had allowed others into her life and it had not been a disaster... she was as proud of herself as she was intrigued by her new found companions.

II.

It had been impossible in the week following the mall trip for Sarah to get the idea of Open Door out of her head. Every time she began an assignment she disliked, she now entertained the idea of substituting it with something she did enjoy, and receiving the school's blessing to do so. It was almost beyond comprehension. She was so intrigued by the concepts that she decided to mention them to Mr. Mahoney. He surely knew of the school, and being a purveyor of true learning, just as surely had an opinion on it. An unrelated to journalism conversation may also allow her to gather how he was holding up and recovering following the incident with Andrew. His classroom demeanor had changed a bit, but he was such a true professional that Sarah doubted anyone but her even noticed. Thursday was issue review day, and class tended to go short, leaving the perfect opportunity to pick his brain.

Preoccupied with fanciful notions of academic freedom, the week flew by. Thursday's issue review went well, and after Mahoney spoke with a student that had not been pulling her weight in getting the issue together, Sarah approached him.

"Mr. Mahoney, I was hoping to talk to you about something." "Anything Sarah. Are you OK?" She immediately quieted his alarm. *"Oh yes. I was just made aware of something very interesting this week and wanted to get an opinion on it. Are you familiar with the Open Door Academy?"* Mahoney smiled, and looked unsurprised. *"I certainly am. It is a fascinating place, and kind of a dirty word amongst the administration here."* He continued, with growing excitement. *"What they offer is remarkable, and so are some of the students they produce. What prompted this question?" "Well, I met a girl that goes there, and she was telling me about how she is allowed to focus on subjects that interest her, and complete assignments in her own way… more than anything she is given the leeway she needs to develop her talents. It just sounds so unfathomable."* Mahoney smiled again. *"It does not surprise me in the slightest that a student of your aptitudes and motivation would be interested in Open Door."* Mahoney paused for what seemed like an hour, and then spoke. *"…Sarah, I don't know if it is too late in the year, but if it is truly a change that you and your parents were interested in making, I would gladly provide the letter of recommendation you would need. Students that don't simply buy their way in need an endorsement letter, of sorts. Almost like a college. I would be sad to see you go; your work here is so exceptional, however I would love to see you develop your interest in writing to its fullest wherever it best suits you."*

Sarah was stunned. None of that was what she expected. She had not even really considered the attending of Open Door as an option, and had put no thought into the logistics that would go into it. She had been so consumed with the methods and learning concepts that Angela had introduced… now she had been offered the possibility of being able to experience them? Her gratefulness to Mahoney would last a lifetime, whether or not the switch to Open Door came to fruition. She would ask her parents and would not bother Mahoney with it again until they had told her for a fact whether it was open to her. The

CHAPTER X

conversation with Mahoney ended on a positive note, and it was very reassuring to hear both his praise of her work and to see him look happy at the prospect of her development. Her parents would likely support any educational ambition she had, especially if they knew that Mr. Mahoney was also behind it. Sarah found herself wanting to talk to Maria and Angela about these developments, but decided to wait until they had established themselves as more than a pipe dream.

It was Maria who approached Sarah about the prospect of a weekend meet-up. Spending time together was talked about, but the mall was not mentioned. It seemed as if the act of socializing was far more important to Maria than the locale. Sarah had not put any thought into where else she would feel comfortable seeing Maria and Angela, and now she had just one day to do so. She would need to finalize a plan with them by the end of school on Friday, or at least she felt that was the courteous thing to do. *"It would just be fun to hang out..."* Maria had said. The prospect of moving too fast was causing Sarah to be leery of a house visit, or a meal, or any other type of one-on-one situation. Her confidence from the previous weekend was largely based on her familiarity and comfort level with the surroundings. She had done alone what her, Maria, and Angela had done literally hundreds of times. The same cannot be said for *"hanging out"* elsewhere. She thought of the possibility of taking them to the Gelato' shop, but that is the only idea she had. There is a chance that she would need to accept the invitation and let the chips fall where they may... leaving the location up to Maria.

Sarah rushed home after school and began straight away on a list of pros and cons to lobby her parents on the Open Door idea. She would wait until dinner was on the table and there

136

were no other distractions present; papers, TV… they could all wait until after she made her case. Her list was impressive, and on the tail of her recent emotional outpouring to them, would sound very convincing. Not wanting the emotional baggage of attending a school where she had watched a classmate burn to death, the very same classmate she had exposed not a month prior as a plagiarist, was a compelling argument on its own.

"Guys, I wanted to talk to you about something." The predictable look of shock when Sarah uttered more than a few words now bathed both their faces. *"I haven't really been able to settle back in at Dyersville High following all the things that have happened. I didn't want to make a big deal out of how I was feeling, but I'm beginning to think it may affect my academics. I've been having a lot of trouble focusing, and I've even been having some flashbacks to the incident in the cafeteria."* Sarah paused for a moment to let that statement sink in and then continued. *"I know it takes time to get over any such thing, I just don't want to wait so long that I ruin the rest of the school year."* She had made her opening statement, and awaited a response. Her mother spoke first. *"I'm glad you came to us with this dear; we are both committed to your success, and to keeping you happy. We know how much you usually enjoy school, so it must have taken a lot for you to come to this point."* Her father was slightly less nurturing. *"Sarah, do you have a suggestion? It sounds like you might feel that Dyersville High is no longer right for you."*

Sarah knew that this is where she must tread lightly. She did not want to sound contrived, or like she was suggesting something quite large like a school transfer on a whim. *"I had been thinking about it with no real plan for a few weeks, and then did some research, talked to Mr. Mahoney, and I would like to look in to the possibility of a move to the Open Door Academy across town. Do you know of it?"* Both of her parents nodded simultaneously. *"We've* read an article about it last month in the Tribune. They did quite a piece on it being one of the most unique learning facilities in the area, and explained a little about how it works. It also went over the price." Her father's tone had changed notably with the last sentence, and her mother was quick to log in. "Honey, your father and I were both impressed with what we read, and even commented to each other how well you might perform in that type of environment, with how grown up you are. How did you find out about it?" "Well, I met a girl who goes there, and she explained how it all works. I was intrigued enough to look into it further, and eventually asked Mr. Mahoney. He knew of it well, and even made the offer to write me the transfer letter if it was something we wanted to pursue. He felt it would be great for me to be able to focus on my strengths and interests." She had played the Mahoney card twice, and that was enough. She didn't want them to inadvertently talk again and her have overstated his interest in the transfer. Her parents looked at each other questioningly, but not expressing any emotion that could be considered negative. Her mother ended this segment of the conversation. "Sarah, we are going to have to talk about this. It is a big decision, but we're glad you brought this up. Seeing your academic performance and happiness suffer is certainly not something we are interested in. We shouldn't be surprised that you have done your own research to fix the problem." Her mother smiled, and looked slyly proud of her resourceful daughter. "We'll talk about it and let you know what we think by the end of the weekend." Sarah thanked them, and remained all but silent for the rest of the meal. She was quietly brimming with excitement… a feeling she was wholly unaccustomed to and was all she could do to contain. She felt as if she might burst or that smoke may pour from her ears if she allowed it. Her legs were bouncing a mile a minute as if she were on idle, ready to speed off as soon as she stood. She finished eating and went to her room. Despite her previous efforts to quiet them, even the outside chance of the boy attending Open Door created a flurry of feelings in her body and mind. As much as she might try to deny it she had a connection with the silent, still faceless stranger, and as fanciful as it may have been, it was a feeling she could not shake.

Friday came and was on its way out when she came upon Maria, and had decided to accept the invitation to hang out. Maria again seemed shocked and elated at the very prospect of Sarah's company, and it made her feel good. It was agreed upon that they would talk on the phone later Saturday morning, and if no other worthwhile options came up, the three would revisit the mall. Sarah did not mention Gelato' but had decided she would suggest it, paired with a walk around the village, as their outing. She felt that the girls would not be put off by the soggy weather and that they might actually like it. The library was kind of like the bookstore in the mall... and provided less but not less interesting fodder for watching. Being in familiar circumstances would allow her to stay confident and remain good company. She dreaded the time when she turned so uncomfortable that either of the others would notice; it was bound to happen, but she could do her best to put it off as long as possible.

Her parents summoned her from her room late Sunday afternoon as if calling her to a board meeting. As they sat together in the living room the anticipation in Sarah's mind was almost physically debilitating. She felt as if her hands were melting through her jeans, and it took almost single minded focus to keep her legs from bouncing. Her parents both looked normal- she was sure that if bad news was on the horizon she would be able to tell by demeanor alone. *"Dear, if the logistics are something that can be overcome this late in the year, and Mr. Mahoney has graciously agreed to give his blessing, we are willing to send you to Open Door. Neither of us can even possibly imagine how traumatic all this has been for you, and we trust that you would not have brought it up if it were not serious. You have never been a child that made a mountain out of a molehill."* Sarah smiled, wanted to explode, and said thank you. *"Sarah, we do not want to make a big case of this, but you know of course that Open Door is a private school and does come at quite a cost. We only bring it up because we want you to know how much we value you and your education."* Her father felt a duty as a responsible adult to bring up the finances. She thanked him graciously and made the partially sad, grateful face that she knew they wanted to see, and that signified her understanding of their gift. *"We will contact the school tomorrow and find out what we do next- I would imagine what we need from you is the letter that Mr. Mahoney offered. I would imagine that is a key part of the enrollment process."* Sarah was now speechless. It was sinking in that she may actually be leaving Dyersville High, and she was so excited that it was upsetting her stomach. Her thirst for knowledge and desire for learning were about to meet their match in an environment that suited her. She had never felt like this before. She looked forward to the future; she looked forward to the following week. She wanted the following days to end- not just so the burdensome time would be behind her, but because there was something new on the horizon; something that merely a week ago was beyond her imagination.

Journalism class couldn't come fast enough on Monday, and Mahoney could tell she was eager to talk to him. He smiled as she approached towards the end of class, and beat her to the punch. *"Your parents have agreed to send you to Open Door?"* She was embarrassed at her transparency, and responded as such. *"I'm a bit easy to read right now, huh? Yes, they said they'd send me. I was hoping you were serious about the recommendation letter?"* *"Of course*

Sarah. As I said, it will be bittersweet. I will truly miss having you in my class. I'll draft something up and give it to you to submit along with the rest of your application. I think your only setback may be the late time of year... most schools, especially private, don't like to accept transfers after Fall." Mahoney looked at her in a warm, sincere way that told her he truly would miss her. He said he would have the letter by the end of the week at latest, and to Sarah in her current state, that seemed like forever.

Distracted, she sat and read in the library to pass the time between school day's end and her parents' arrival home from work. She was eager to hear what they had found out and if the timing coincided with Mahoney's. She would transfer tomorrow if it were possible, even if it meant she had to start the year from scratch. Now that the idea was firmly planted in her head it seemed that there was no stopping it.

Literally meeting her parents in the driveway, they too could tell she had an agenda. *"Dear, I spoke with Open Door today, and I have some mixed news. The good news is that based on the situation that occurred at Dyersville High they have opened several late transfer spots to Dyersville students. The bad news is that there are four students applying for two spots, you being the fourth. They are collecting applications this week and said they would make sorting it out a high priority. We should expect an answer, assuming we get the letter from Mr. Mahoney on time, by early next week."* Sarah was unsure how to react. She said thank you, and then began to return to reality and deal with the fact that she may not get chosen and will remain at Dyersville High. She should have expected nothing less, but the plan seemed so solid that she made the mistake of getting her hopes up. Her excitement briefly turned to anger and she went to her room to look at the stars. Her academic performance was spotless, her recommendation from Mahoney would be shining… the only potential blemish would be the incident with Carlson and Heffernan and whether it had actually been left off her record. If that became what tipped the scales, she thought, Carlson and Heffernan would surely be made to share her pain. There was nothing left to do now but wait, and hope.

III.

The week in the hospital had been tedious, but Simon's recovery was going well. He used the time to read and get his head right, knowing that upon returning to Wolcott neither his actions nor demeanor could show anything out of the ordinary. He knew that he would be the unwilling center of attention and must not let it veer him off path. The same people that would feign care for his well-being after the incident couldn't have cared less about him before, just as he couldn't care less about them now. The only difference is now they know something about him, which was a fact he could do nothing but accept.

He had several new scars from the incident, and all but one was in a semi-conspicuous place; eyebrow, chin, and a crooked horseshoe shape on the side of his head. With stitches newly removed, the skin was still bright pink and stuck out as if it were intentionally illuminated. His ribs had not even begun to feel better, and he would be required to wear a cast on his hand for at least another two weeks, possibly more. The hand he could deal with- if the occasion arose his cast could be used as a weapon- however the ribs were a huge liability. He couldn't run, and he could barely stand upright without pain pills. Even with the elastic wrap the doctor had given him to stabilize the area, he was in constant pain, and his movement was severely restricted. He usually tried to avoid doing so at school but upon his return he would be forced to arm himself. Either a boot knife or something tucked inconspicuously into his waistband would be mandatory. Weapons of any kind were banned on school grounds for obvious reasons, however he had smuggled several knives into his room taped inside his shoes at the start of this semester. They were placed strategically under his bed, where without thorough visual inspection they would never be found, but allowing him to reach them immediately if necessary. The thought had crossed his mind during the incident- how quickly and completely he could have changed the course of it, and how dramatically his life would have been altered afterwards. Accepting the beating was necessary, and revenge could be addressed at a later date. For now he had to focus on being released from the hospital and getting back on his path of engineering his exit from Wolcott-North.

"How are you feeling today Simon?" Dr. Wells had been in at least twice a day for the entire time he had been there, and he had seen Nurse Vanessa much more frequently. He was grateful for their attentiveness, if only for the fact that he truly wanted to get better and get out, and needed their help. *"I'm feeling much better Doctor. My ribs still hurt, but everything else is doing fine. Vanessa took my stitches out this morning, and my hand has stopped throbbing completely." "How is your head? Everything else will heal, son, but we need to be cautious of that concussion."* Simon had been feeling dizzy every day since the incident in slightly lessening degrees. *"It feels fine... I was feeling a bit fuzzy the first few days, but it's gone away now. Now I'm just restless."* He smiled, as if to indicate a joke, but Wells brushed it off in lieu of trying to determine Simon's forthrightness regarding his condition. Simon had taken caution to act as normal and unaffected by his injuries as possible whenever the doctor was present, knowing that the

duration of his stay rested directly in his hands. The doctor had no reason not to believe what Simon said, but still seemed reluctant to let him go. *"Let's give it until tomorrow afternoon."* Dr. Wells stated resolutely. *"It will give you another day to rest, and us another day to watch you. I don't want to risk your injuries worsening because we wanted to hurry you out of here."* Simon was disappointed, but not surprised. He still looked a mess with the fresh scars, black eyes, and casted hand. His posture was awful as he felt the need to slouch to favor his ribs. One more day of recuperation wasn't the end of the world. A case could be made that the longer he was forced to stay in the hospital, the more severe the attack would seem, and the more leverage he could squeeze out of it.

Simon's body appreciated the rest. He fell asleep listening to a conversation between a patient and a night nurse that was occurring in the hallway in front of his room and didn't wake until after 9am. The nurse was made aware of his impending release and needed to check vitals, eyesight, and generally give him a once-over before the doctor made his final evaluation that afternoon. *"We'll miss having you around here Simon. You are a model patient."* Nurse Vanessa said with a smile. *"You haven't complained once about the food, other patients, needles, cold hands… I wish I could clone you!"* Simon would miss her nurturing, caring demeanor; she was the only one in his life in the past several years that had exhibited that sort of behavior towards him, and it made him feel close to her. She truly made the trying experience of being cooped up in the hospital a tolerable one. He wanted to thank her, but aside from a simple voicing of the sentiment, did not know how. *"You have been so nice to me, and I wanted to say thank you."* Vanessa looked a little surprised at the break from his neutral demeanor. *"Well you're certainly welcome. I mean this in the nicest possible way, but I hope I don't see you again!"*

Again she smiled, leaving Simon with the notion that he would likely never see her again, but she would be on his mind. The list of people that treated him lovingly was a very short one, and the attention was not lost on him.

She gave him a clean bill of health, or at least clean enough to warrant a release. His vision was still a little shaky, and he struggled a bit with the eye test, but made it through. Pending his doctor visit he was as good as out. Dr. Wells came in around 12:30pm, looked Simon over, reviewed the nurse's chart, and bid him farewell with little fanfare. He warned Simon of any premature activity in his condition, and told him he would see him in two to three weeks to take the cast off. What Dr. Wells lacked in warmth and bedside manner, Vanessa had more than made up for. He was ready to go and now just needed to call the school to come get him. The next phase of his recovery would be the difficult one.

Wolcott sent a van, and Simon felt some slight panic during the ride back to school. The nervousness he was feeling was a combination of feeling physically weak and not knowing if his escape plans would work as seamlessly as he hoped. He was not the sort that unduly questioned himself, but sitting alone in the back seat of a strange-smelling school van as if being privately escorted to his own execution, the self-doubt crept in. His stomach turned as they entered the driveway at Wolcott. He thanked the driver, who did not respond, and began the walk back to his room. He was given no instructions to check in with anyone, he was not greeted by any administrators. He had his backpack *(which had been brought to him early in his stay)*, a small bag of pain medication, and his bloody clothes, still unwashed from the night of the beating. He took a big deep breath upon arriving at the door to his room prior to entering.

Much to his surprise it had been straightened, and there was no
visual evidence of the altercation. He had fully expected to find
the room in the same disarray as when he last saw it- things
strewn about, blood on the floor- but someone had cleaned it.
He put his bag down and immediately checked under his bed
for his knives. They were unmoved, and he was very glad he
had taken such precautions in hiding them. Promptly wedging
his desk chair under the door handle, Simon enjoyed his first
moments of privacy in over a week. Since no one had even
acknowledged his return, he felt no pressure to attend 7th and
8th period. He would take the afternoon off, catch up on some
unfinished homework, and begin again tomorrow. If he
attended the last *(and usually least crowded)* dinner block, he
would likely not see any of his attackers until hallway passing
tomorrow. He was positive that one more night of solid rest,
especially in the privacy of his own room, would do wonders
for his recovery.

Walking to dinner was an eye-opening experience. Everyone he
passed by shot him a knowing glance- some supportive, some
sympathetic, several hostile. There was obviously a story
circulating about what had happened, and it was also obvious
people had taken sides on it. Now armed, he felt confident that
if things were to go south again he would certainly stand a
chance of defending himself even in his weakened state. He
was tempted to put his hood up, but did not want to seem as if
he felt victimized. He walked confidently through the dinner
line, found a seat with his back to a wall, and ate slowly. The
food at Wolcott was not anything to speak of, but it was
certainly better than the hospital. Prying eyes flashed towards
him frequently during his meal. More acutely aware of his own
presence than usual, he was feeling self-conscious and very
exposed. He took great care to go unnoticed in all situations,

and right now he had absolutely no chance of doing so. All he could do was look away in order to avoid attempts at conversation.

One of his peers ignored the social cue he was putting forth and approached him brazenly. It was a boy he had seen around and knew as a member of the track team and a math standout. *"You're Simon, right?"* Simon nodded reluctantly. *"Man, I heard that you might have brain damage. That's why you were gone for so long. You don't, do you?"* Almost incapable of answering such a stupid question in a respectful way, Simon replied simply. *"Um, no. No I don't have brain damage."* He fixed his gaze on the boy in a way that was geared to make him uncomfortable, but it was ignored. *"Dude, what did you do to those guys to make them that angry? I mean, they kicked the shit out of you."* Feeling dizzy and impatient, Simon barked *"Nothing. I did nothing."* He stood up, continued to stare at his inquisitor, and the hint finally got through. *"OK man, well I was just curious."* The boy scurried off, and Simon dreaded the thought of dealing with this level of social interaction until the novelty of his situation had worn off. Walking back to his room, he carried his sweatshirt over his casted arm in an effort to be less conspicuous. From 10 yards his other injuries were not visible, but the cast was a giveaway from any distance. Simply arriving at his room felt like an accomplishment, and the evening alone with his thoughts felt like a prize he had earned in a grueling week-long contest.

IV.

Lisi spotted Simon immediately during the walk to his first period class. Wholeheartedly faking a look of interest as to his well-being and compassion towards his situation, he approached Simon. *"Mr. Ravenhall, it is good to see you back here, and looking well on your way to recovery. We were all shocked at what happened to you, and please rest assured, all avenues are being looked at in order to identify the guilty parties. We don't take that kind of thing lightly here at Wolcott."* The vision Simon had of drawing the blade from his waist and shoving it into the lower abdomen of the dirty, two-faced liar standing in front of him was so vivid he had to blink twice to shake it off. He replied with a smile. *"I'm sure you're doing what you can to find the students that did this to me. I'm just concerned with getting better and not letting my grades slip while doing so. I guess the sports option is out for a while, huh?"* Simon regretted the backhanded joke as soon as he put it out there, and Lisi gave him a look that confirmed why. *"I guess so Simon. I hope you use your recovery time as a time to learn and grow, and not just further remove yourself from Wolcott society. People don't respond well to things or people they don't understand."* If Lisi was good at one thing, it was saying something without actually saying it. In both of their conversations, Simon left feeling as if he was meant to be intimidated, and he hoped that Lisi left feeling like he was unsuccessful in doing so. *"I'm going to make sure I look out for myself a little better on all fronts, since no one here is going to do it for me."* Simon smiled again, then turned and left. The final jab at Lisi was not so subtle, was not meant to be, and was intended to put him off. He wanted to create an atmosphere in which he was a liability that the faculty did not want to deal with and would be grateful to have out of their hair. Ruffling someone as high up the food chain as Lisi would be a great start. Letting the boys that beat him know that *he* knew was the next step.

He was approached several more times throughout the day- the general tone being one of surprise, especially once they got up close and saw the damage that had been done. One girl named Betsy said that she had seen him wheeled out into the ambulance and had been feeling worried and unsettled since.

She had a warmth to her that felt much like Nurse Vanessa, and Simon did not mind her interjection into his privacy. All the others bothered him and treated him like a novelty to be gawked at, but the girl looked at him with genuine concern and relief. The comforting feeling did not last long, as he saw the first of his attackers moving in his direction down the hall. He had rehearsed the plan in his head, and hoped it went the same in reality. The boy undoubtedly noticed him, and Simon stepped laterally directly into his path. The boy had no choice but to stop in the crowded hallway, and Simon demanded his attention by glaring directly into his eyes. The boys' eyes shifted, but Simon would not let him look away. *"How are you Scott?"* Simon asked coldly. *"I'm fine. Can I help you?"* Simon inched closer. *"Oh no. I just wanted to compliment you on your work."* Simon tilted his head in a direction that brought the deep, horseshoe-shaped scab on the side of his head into full view. Scott looked as if he was going to respond, but Simon darted his gaze back into his eyes and the boy stammered and moved nervously away. He would no doubt tell the others of the incident, and that would make his next two encounters a little more challenging. Simon had obviously caught this one by surprise, and would not have that luxury with the other two. The eyes that he had peered into today were not the brazen, fiery ones that he had seen the night of his attack. They were meek and breakable and most of all scared. He had taken their worst and had come back. He knew who they were, and had not the slightest reservation about letting them know. The free pass they seem to have been given by the administration would not be replicated by Simon. The innocuous confrontations in the school hallway were just the beginning.

Lunch period was almost always a noisy, cluttered affair. The social segregation that was not allowed in other facets of the

Wolcott-North lifestyle was unavoidable and prevalent during grazing time. Simon placed himself safely in a corner with his back to the wall and waited for the second and third boys to enter the cafeteria and be seated with their meals. He truly did not know the identity of the fourth, but expected that after shaking up the other three, it would not take much to figure out. The boys entered, went through the line, and seated themselves in regular fashion with the other well-to-do athletes and pseudo-high-society pricks. One was named David, and the other he was not sure of. He was almost sure it was David who had shoved him in the hallway prior to the attack, and was more than sure that the two boys seated next to each other were in his room that night. A physical body can be covered and masked, but eyes, and guilt, are unmistakable.

Simon picked at his lunch and then approached the table. The boys saw him coming and tried to laugh it off as a joke amongst themselves. They were looking anywhere but at Simon, and probably expected some over-the-top showing of bravado that would be easily dismissed as childish and non-threatening. Simon approached the table, ignoring everyone in the world except the two boys sitting next to each other and now just mere feet from him. They finally looked up as he finished his approach, and seemed shocked when he squatted down beside them and placed his casted hand on the nearest boys' leg. Simon did not say a word for probably most of a minute, and the strangeness of it all was too much for David. *"What do you want man? Do we know you?"* Simon smiled as if he were about to begin devouring them alive. *"Oh, sure you do. You know me better than most. I just wanted to come over and say hello. Make sure that we stayed in touch, you know."* The boys were not laughing now, and Simon's gaze shifted back and forth between them to ensure their full attention. He remained quiet and motionless with his hand resting on the nameless one's leg for another period of time. Positive that he had their attention, Simon reached up to the fresh scab with his free hand and peeled away a large piece of it, letting the blood flow down the side of his head. The boys' breath became notably urgent, and with a practiced quickness, Simon reached up, swiped some blood off his head, and wiped it on the pants of the nameless boy. The boy shot up out of his seat and backed away from Simon, looking appalled and a bit queasy. Simon rose slowly and said *"Now you two have a good day, OK?"* Simon smeared the blood remaining in his hand onto his cast, and the boys could not take their eyes off it. The table was silent, and the rest of the lunch room had continued, business as usual. Simon's head hurt immensely in the spot where he had removed the fresh scab, but his facial expression did not change as he had done so. His gaze stayed fixed on his targets, and when he stopped in the restroom and saw the volume of blood that had poured from the scar, he was sure he had made the intended impression.

Simon was surprised that it took three days, but the call came during 5th period on Friday for him to report to Lisi's office. Lisi was not the principal, or the vice principal, but had obviously been assigned to Simon for some reason. It was possible the administration thought he might be able to relate to him, or possibly make a dent in forcing his extroversion. As he walked to Lisi's office, he imagined this being the point at which patience were lost. Lisi didn't seem the sort that dealt well with not getting his way, and he was certainly not getting it with Simon. Frustration would likely come quickly, especially on the heels of his exploits over the past few days.

Lisi was waiting for him behind the desk, looking solemn, and grasping a stack of papers covered by a manila folder. *"Simon, please sit down."* It was obvious from the get-go that this was the no-nonsense version of Lisi. The disingenuous, nurturing, advice-giving father-figure was not here today. Simon sat, being sure to look confident and unwavering as Lisi looked up from the stack of papers at the still scarred student seated before him. *"What are we going to do with you Simon?"* Lisi asked, as if he expected some sort of answer. *"I'm not sure what you mean, I'm afraid."* Simon responded. Lisi snapped back. *"You know* exactly *what I mean!* Playing *innocent does not* make *you innocent, son. Don't toy with me."* The frustration was finally coming out, and Simon was ready for it. *"I don't feel I'm guilty of anything, sir. And I'm not your son."* Lisi's eyebrows narrowed and he glared at Simon. *"You have no grounds to threaten any students here. We have not come to any conclusions about whom it was that attacked you, and it is not your place to make assumption. Do you understand?"* *"No I don't."* Simon said indignantly. *"I have not threatened anyone- I've barely spoken to anyone since my return. I have said hello to a few friends, and several people have wished me well in my recovery, but that is it. I don't know where you're getting your information, but it is false."* Lisi looked incensed. *"Boy, I have been at this school for 23 years- longer than you have been alive- and I know your kind. Too smart for your own good and not experienced enough in life to understand when you're making a mistake. I'm trying to help you, and my first piece of advice is not to ruffle feathers around here. Do you understand?"* Simon felt Lisi's hardened facade cracking. *"You keep asking me if I understand, and I do not. In our previous meeting you told me to become more involved in the Wolcott lifestyle, and now I'm being chastised for an attempt at socializing? No. I do not understand."* Lisi slammed both hands down on the desk, sending a pencil and a small tin of paper clips flying. *"You do not know it was those boys that attacked you! Leave them alone and let the school do its job in identifying your attackers! That is an order!"* Lisi was speaking to him in a harsh and hateful tone, and Simon made it a point to remain stoic. He thought intently about his next words. He waited a few moments for Lisi to speak again, but he did not. He just glared at Simon with his hands still resting in the positions he had slammed them into. *"I don't know who you are referring to when you say* "those boys"*, and I don't know how I could possibly leave anyone here any* more *alone. You've been misled, Mr. Lisi, and I don't know for what purpose, but it is not my problem. If I want to talk to a student, I will talk to them. Do* you *understand?"* Lisi backhanded a coffee mug off his desk and it smashed on the floor. "GET OUT! *You disrespectful, ungrateful lout!"*

Simon kept his eyes fixed on Lisi's, and rose to his feet. He stood still and stared at the selfish egomaniac of a man standing in front of him and thought about how many children he had misguided to further his own gains, how many had genuinely needed his help, and been fed the same rigmarole that Simon had. Lisi may as well have been his fourth attacker. As Simon turned and left, he felt very much like he had opened an un-closable door. It would have to be well planned, but he needed to go over Lisi's head and make sure that someone was aware of the events of the day. It was time for him to go- to leave Wolcott- and he was doing everything in his power to sneakily but thoroughly wear out his welcome.

Over the course of the next days he was contacted by two different guidance counselors, one male and one female, each wanting to assure he had *"emotionally recovered"* from the incident. They both stated that they knew how difficult it must be to return to normal after such a thing, and expressed how eager they were to help put this nasty business behind him. In the interest of sowing the seeds of departure as deep as he could, he accepted both appointments. Ms. Davis was a 40-something heavy-set woman, and naturally gifted with the sympathetic doe-eyes that her job called for. Upon entry, she surveyed Simon and looked as if she wanted to give him a big hug. He did not trust the sentiment as genuine, but appreciated the effort.

"Mr. Ravenhall, thank you for meeting with me. I'm sorry it's been a week since your return and we're just now getting together." The timing was of no surprise to Simon- it was undoubtedly a direct result of the failed meeting with Lisi. *"Simon, everyone is so sorry for what happened to you. Are you feeling any better?"* Simon had no intention of answering on behalf of his physical condition. *"Not really, Ms. Davis. Most of the students have made me feel like some sort of circus freak, and just last week Mr. Lisi chastised me for speaking with students and then yelled at me. I'm not really feeling much better at all. I feel unsafe, and I think that people know who did this to me and are not doing anything about it. It's all very unsettling."* Ms. Davis looked bewildered. It was clear that she was not expecting that level of information, and was unprepared for it. *"Well… that is certainly a lot to deal with. Certainly. I am shocked to hear that Mr. Lisi yelled at you, and I can guarantee that if the faculty knew who the boys were that attacked you, they would be punished. I can see how you're feeling very insecure right now, but rest assured…"* Simon interrupted. *"Ms. Davis, I'm not feeling insecure. The things I've said happened, happened. I do not want to talk to Mr. Lisi anymore, nor should I be expected to. He is not looking out for me, and based on our conversation I believe he knows who attacked me."*

Ms. Davis, just as her counterpart had the week before, turned on him. *"Simon, what you have suggested is very serious, and I will not let you sit here and slander a well-respected member of our staff. I think we should set up a meeting with you, Mr. Lisi, and myself and get to the*

154

bottom of all this. I know this has been hard for you, but…" Again Simon jumped in. "But what, Ms. Davis? I should just move on, and act as if everything is OK? I will not meet with Mr. Lisi and I also do not want to be at this school any more. I don't trust anyone here, and will not be able to learn in this environment." The counselor looked flustered. She remained silent for a few moments, and then responded. "Sometimes things happen that we cannot control, and all we can do is make the best of what happens next. If you do not feel that Wolcott-North is the place for you anymore, and your advisors agree, then we can take further steps. For now, please try to peacefully coexist with the students here and let me know if there is anything else I can do to help." She smiled, and although it was as fake as the interest Lisi expressed in helping him, he respected her composure. He had meant to come off as believable, yet a bit unhinged, and inconsolable. He did not want them to think this was something he would get over and seamlessly rejoin the Wolcott idiot parade.

Time outside class was spent almost exclusively in his room at this point, save some walks around campus at dusk. He was always at full alert, and although it felt good to be outside, his current physical anxiety made it less enjoyable. He had seen each of the boys several times since approaching them, and they would not so much as glance his way. He knew that it was a bit of a conspiracy theory, but he truly pictured Lisi instructing them to go out of their way to ignore and avoid him until something could be done. There was not one doubt in Simon's mind that Lisi knew the identities of the boys that attacked him- the only variable was whether he was advising them now. They had surely come to him after Simon had approached them, leading to the meeting, but had it ended there? He doubted it. They were some of Lisi's golden boys- his "model students"- and worth protecting. Without the extracurricular involvement that Lisi had suggested, Simon was a throw-away. Straight A's did not bring accolades like a sports title, or a student that went on to sports scholarship in college. It was a lesson learned hard, but one that Simon used as motivation.

Ms. Davis contacted him again late Thursday afternoon and requested a Monday morning meeting in her office. Simon accepted, and spent the next few days with piqued curiosity as to the topic. He had met briefly with Mr. LaRue, the male guidance counselor, but chose to stay on topic and play by the rules. He had blasted a rather large path over the past week or so and was cautious to not seem *completely* unhinged or irrational, or worst of all, out to get Lisi. He needed to be cautious of the boy's club that was the Wolcott-North academy. He did not have parents that would come running to his rescue if he got in over his head. All he wanted was a clean break, not an all-out war.

Simon walked directly from breakfast in the cafeteria to his meeting with Ms. Davis. He was five minutes early and heard her talking to someone quietly inside her office. Assuming that he was next in line he waited to see the door open and another student come out. Instead, he was called in through a partially opened door, and was shocked to see Lisi and Dean Hardison both seated in the room. *"We did not mean to trick you Simon, but based on our conversation last week I did not think you would cooperate if I told you that Mr. Lisi was going to be present."* Simon was caught off guard, and speechless. He sat down, folded his arms as best he could while wearing the still blood-covered cast, and remained silent. *"Simon, I am Dean William Hardison. We haven't met personally, but I know you've seen me around. I have been brought up to speed on what has transpired here, and most importantly, I am very sorry for what happened to you."* Simon thanked him simply, and waited for the next speaker to buzz in. *"In our meeting the other day, you brought up some very troubling issues. We are not going to address them one by one- there is no need to rehash a difficult conversation- but I wanted to say that I have spoken with Mr. Lisi about them, and he assures me that you are mistaken on all fronts."* Ms. Davis had spoken on Lisi's behalf with him present in the room as if she was his lawyer, and Simon looked at Lisi with disgust. Lisi would not look back at him.

"I have discussed your feeling that Wolcott-North is no longer right for you with both Dean Hardison and Mr. Lisi. Due to the highly irregular nature of what has happened to you, we are willing to support you in switching schools if you truly feel you can no longer effectively learn and interact here. We have contacted your parents and told them all that has transpired, and they have agreed to respect your wishes regarding a transfer. Is that what you want Simon?" With no pause at all, Simon responded. *"I want to be out of here as soon as possible, Ms. Davis. Yes, that is definitely what I want."* He again looked at Lisi with as much disdain as he could summon, and Dean Hardison noticed and tried to ease the tension. *"Simon, even if you do leave here, I want you to know that we value you as a student, and that everyone in this room has done their best to look out for all the students here. What happened to you was the first time in the history of this school that a student needed medical care after a scuffle. We could not be more sorry, and will do everything we can to ease the headache of a transfer."* Expressing the sentiment in Lisi's presence made it almost completely unbelievable, but nonetheless a relief that not even the Dean would be obstructing his path out of there. He didn't know where he would go, and he didn't care. Anywhere but Wolcott, and as soon as fucking possible.

Over the next week he was asked to sign a variety of papers

regarding his transfer, had met with Ms. Davis again to discuss a timeline, and even had several phone conversations with his parents. Public school was not an option, and the only other live-in academy was boys only, and almost 40 miles away. Simon's parents had a small house on the outskirts of Dyersville, a town nearby the Wolcott campus, and there were several private day-schools in the area. Based on Simon's academic aptitude and social idiosyncrasies, Ms. Davis had recommended one called the Open Door Academy. She described it to Simon and his parents as a progressive learning environment, and seemingly well-suited to Simon's personality. It was an ambitious walk from Simon's parent's house, but the prospect of walking to and from school and having the time afterwards to himself was beyond exciting. With the strong blessing from Wolcott, and the financial support of his parents, he was assured that admission halfway through his 9th grade year would not be a problem. Within the week he would be on his way to putting the Wolcott-North Academy behind him.

The small house in Dyersville was essentially empty, as his parents only spent a week or two a year there, and purchased it as an investment property in a growing, affluent neighborhood. The school was unaware that Simon would be living on his own, and he had specifically asked his parents to keep that fact to themselves when speaking with both schools. A boy of his age living on his own in most cases would be a huge mistake, but the only other choice besides another boarding school was for Simon to move around with his parents, and it was made clear *(although not directly spoken)* that *that* option was not available. His parents had said they would send a cleaning lady in once a week both to keep the house straight and to do the shopping. Simon was required to send his parents the mail that came to the house, and keep himself healthy and safe- nothing more. Now that they could not pay for his life up-front and periodically throughout the school year, they had agreed to send him a credit card for incidental expenses.

It was a week until they heard back from the Open Door Academy. Much to Simon's relief, and surely that of everyone else involved as well, he was granted the transfer. He would finish out the week at Wolcott-North, move over the weekend, and begin at Open Door the following Monday. All the physical and mental anguish of the past months had been worth it. He was proud of himself for strategically engineering his way out of a terrible situation, even if it meant enduring another terrible situation. He would need to use all the focus he could muster to stay on track for the next four days at Wolcott, and to go as unnoticed as possible. His plans for dealing with those that had hurt him hinged completely on letting them think he had forgotten and moved on.

Simon used the remaining days to study intently and finish all current homework, projects, and the remainder of the work he had missed while in the hospital. He wanted to transfer to Open Door at the top of his academic game, not allowing the distractions of the previous weeks to derail him. He was assured all his grades and credits would be transferred, he would begin at the same point in the year, and would move into classes as similar as available to the ones he had left. It seemed almost too good to be true.

Physically he was feeling better- his ribs were no longer a constant nagging pain- and he was sure the cast was ready to be removed from his arm. His scabs *(with the exception of the one he damaged)* were healing nicely, and there was a possibility he would look mostly normal upon starting his new school. He had an appointment on Thursday afternoon to see Dr. Wells, and was hoping to leave cast-less, and with a clean bill of health. He knew that he needed to shop over the weekend- his only non-uniform clothes were old and the pants were a little short. He was less than 48 hours from freedom, and in his mind he was already gone.

Simon was walking from lunch to the first of his afternoon classes when a strange feeling rolled over him. Not a second later he was shoved from behind just as he had been prior to the attack. He did not turn around, and did not need to. He stopped in his tracks, slid his hand to his waist, and waited. *"We heard you're leaving, you freak"* said the nameless boy from the cafeteria. *"We just wanted to say how sorry we are that you're going. There won't be anyone left to beat on."* He recognized the second voice as that of David, and was shocked at the brazenness of his confession. Simon was angry, but knew that it was not the time to act on it. To take both boys on in his current state he would need to draw his weapon, and that would change everything. He remained face forward, accepted another shove from David, and waited. The bell rang for class and they scattered.

Antagonizing him at this point was futile. He made sure to wedge his desk chair underneath the door handle for the last few nights of his captivity, just in case, but no commotion ever came. His cast was removed on Thursday by Nurse Vanessa, and Friday rolled along with very little fanfare. He met one last time with Ms. Davis, mostly just as a formality, and then it ended. When the final bell rang on Friday afternoon it echoed in his mind as if it were a summoning from beyond. He had already packed all his things and waited for the cab seated on the front steps of the magnificent stone main building. He thought back through his time at Wolcott, and was left questioning how different his life might have been had he grown up somewhere else. All his struggles, all his successes, all his growth, all spent by himself. He had existed for years in his own mind, and now he would finally get to experience what he thought may have been out there for him all along. It was if he were being released from prison, but never had a normal life prior to his incarceration. Everything would be new, everything would be real. Wolcott, for all it was, was not real. It was a contrived, manipulated reality that created warped values and an even more warped sense of self-importance. Even at the formative age of 14, and just halfway through the 9th grade, Simon could grasp those realities with the utmost clarity.

He was leaving it all behind with not a single reservation or regret, and vowed never to take for granted his new and hard-earned gift of freedom.

CHAPTER XI.

The agony of suspense regarding Sarah's admission to Open
Door was overshadowed, albeit only slightly, by her feelings of
elation after reading the recommendation letter from Mr.
Mahoney. It read like a fairy tale... praising not only her work
but her insight, depth of interest in her studies, and even her
caring demeanor in the face of the situation with Andrew.
These were things that she never fathomed anyone would
notice, let alone take the care to mention. It was a well-written
three paragraphs, and it truly made her seem like a student
deserving of the special treatment she had requested. Reading
it made her regretful of the prospect of leaving Mahoney's
class, but also excited at the potential for progress; if a teacher
of his caliber had seen all these qualities in her, the teachers at
Open Door would surely appreciate her as well. She was also
excited about leaving Dyersville High before something
happened that she could *truly* not come back from. The
elaborateness of her ruse regarding the Andrew Mahoney
incidents had easily thrown people off her trail, but who knows
with continued exposure for another year and a half of school

if the facade would hold up. She was poised to leave Mahoney with him being infallible in her eyes, and was grateful that she would never take the chance of the true respect and admiration she felt towards him being tarnished.

Tuesday evening when she returned home her mother greeted her with a smile on her face. She held in her hand the acceptance letter from the Open Door Academy. They wrote that she had been chosen based not only on academic prowess but on her integrity and character as outlined in Mahoney's recommendation letter. They had high hopes for her, they said, and pending a smooth mid-year transition, the remainder of her 11th grade year was sure to be an exciting and productive time. They included a temporary ID card, a class list, and a booklet explaining the ins and outs of Open Door's policies and procedures. She would finish the week at Dyersville and begin her new adventure on Monday. It was time to tell Mahoney, and it was also time to tell Maria and Angela.

She passed Maria in the halls on several occasions throughout the day, and they would always exchange knowing glances and warm smiles. Only due to time constraints did they not stop more frequently to talk. Today, Sarah made sure to find her during her lunch period, and broke the news to her. *"Maria, I have something to tell you!"* To see Sarah excited was a true anomaly, and Maria reacted as such. *"Well it appears to be good news… tell me!"* Slowing down just enough to catch her breath and assess Maria's reaction, she continued. *"Well, after talking with Angela, and then Mr. Mahoney, I applied for a transfer to Open Door, and was accepted! I'll be finishing the week here and starting there next Monday!"* She was met with a strange reaction from Maria… kind of a half-smile with a very visible underlying note of sadness. *"I'm happy for you Sarah. I'm sorry I reacted this way; it's just that it's nice to see you here every day. It helps me feel normal."* Sarah had not even considered that with Angela already at another school that Maria was rather isolated here, and her leaving would further do so. She was valued as a friend- another foreign feeling that she had not prepared for. *"I'm sorry, I didn't mean to be so braggy about it, I just found out last night and couldn't wait to tell you."* Sarah needed to make her feel valued right now, and her statement seemed to have worked. *"Really? Well, I'm glad you told me, I'm just sad to lose a friend here."* Sarah came back immediately. *"You were the first person I told! I haven't even told Mr. Mahoney yet! ...you're not losing me as a friend... with a little more time to get my school work done during the week my weekends will be even more free than they are now. And I'll watch over Angela for you."* Sarah finished with a big smile. Maria smiled back, seemingly reassured by the conversation. *"Congratulations Sarah... from everything Angela tells me about the school, you'll do amazing there."* And then it happened- Maria hugged Sarah. It was unexpected to say the least, and Sarah did not know how to react. She pulled back momentarily and unintentionally, but immediately upon realizing how rude it was, relaxed and hugged her back. It felt nice.

She thought quickly about the last time she had been touched by anyone, and it had been quite some time. Her mother's hand on her back during consolation over the events with Andrew had been the last time, and that was a mere brush. She had not been touched by anyone besides her mother, ever. She was kind of embarrassed by her feelings, and felt she may have held on to the hug for a little too long. Maria did not seem the slightest bit put off, and looked happy as they parted and vowed to talk later in the week. Sharing her news with Maria was a much more emotional event than expected, but also made her feel even more confident about the change, as she now knew that she would have a confidant to talk to about her new adventure. Try as she might, she also could not get the powerful feelings the hug had generated out of her mind.

Telling Mahoney the news was bittersweet. It was clear that he was both proud and distressed, and the sadness was obvious on his face. Sarah made him aware that it was his letter that had tipped the scales, and to that fact he put on a humble smile that moved Sarah to reach out and hug him. He pulled back much as she had when Maria hugged her, and then briefly hugged her back. There was no one in class, Sarah made sure of it, as she knew that teacher/student contact was forbidden. Mr. Mahoney told her that if she ever needed anything, even down to an opinion on a story or assignment, that she could contact him. She had two days left in his class, but for all intents and purposes, this was goodbye. He had been easily the most influential figure in her young life, and she felt he had set the bar almost unattainably high for those to follow.

She floated through her walk home, feeling a combination of excitement and anticipation, and the space was shared with unusual feelings of warmth directed at her new friends. She had experienced more physical contact today than she had in her entire life; it left her with a sense of vulnerability, but also one of closeness to both Maria and Mahoney. She had so much to think about; she had so much ahead of her. For the first time she had ambition and vision for the future, replacing what was usually just the dull ache of confusion and maladjustment. She had feelings of hope where before there had been none. It made her feel full even though she had not eaten all day, and warm even though she was under-dressed for such a long walk in the blustery weather.

The remainder of the week had breezed by. Several of her teachers had been made aware of her departure and shared words of encouragement and offered praise of her performance in their classes. Being noticed in such a way was nice, and she was worried that she was using it all up in one week. She met with a guidance counselor on Friday morning regarding the transfer of her records, and after briefly seeing Maria during lunch period, the day seemed to end as if she were in a daze. She did, however, remember Journalism- Mr. Mahoney had said a few words about her during class, and they were well-received and echoed by many of her classmates. Several students asked if she was OK, and several others expressed their jealousy, also having heard great things about Open Door. She collected the items she needed from her locker, turned in her books at the library as per the request of the guidance counselor, and walked out the doors of Dyersville High for presumably the last time. Her thoughts were a whirlwind of Andrew Mahoney, her writing, her new friendships, and her new emotional vulnerability. She flashed back to her time in 9th grade, when she would literally go entire days without uttering a word, and was proud of the accomplishment. She felt no less strange and the darkness inside her was no less alive, but the past two years had taught her that projecting those feelings outwardly would lead to nothing but alienation and trouble. She had successfully adapted to her environment, and yet still maintained her devotion to righting the wrongs she saw in it. She still felt the fear and ominousness that had always surrounded her, but she had begun to build a barrier to keep them at bay so they did not rule her life. She *had* learned lessons in high school, just perhaps not the conventional ones.

II.

The temporary solution to the problem of Open Door being too far for even an ambitious walk was for Sarah's mother to drop her off on her way to work. The shift in her morning schedule was going to be an adjustment, but the excitement of what lay ahead overshadowed all. Her mother talked to her throughout the entire car ride on Monday morning, but none of it made it through. Sarah was completely preoccupied, and had taken great care to ensure that she was prepared for the day in every conceivable way. The mental checklist in her brain was on repeat, and drowned out any words of wisdom or encouragement her mother had put forth. Care was taken with her outfit, her lunch, the contents of her backpack, her writing utensils… nothing was left to chance. Nothing she did was coincidental or without forethought. She was entering a realm of higher learning, and she needed to rise to the occasion.

The car ride was over and she was in front of the Open Door Academy for the first time. She had studied the literature; she had prepared her desired class list. Her first order of business was a meeting with a student counselor named Mr. Travers. She entered the doors with a knot the size of a heart in her stomach, and the first person she saw was the security guard Charles, who greeted her with a warm smile that let her know that *he* knew she had arrived for her first day. *"Hello Ma'am. How can I help you today?"* She was taken with the paradox of his appearance and his persona. A truly frightening looking figure, he couldn't have seemed more caring if he tried. *"Hello, and thank you. Today is my first day, and I'm supposed to meet with Mr. Travers."* He nodded slowly *"Things aren't too busy up here, let me walk you there."* Sarah was grateful for the escort, as one of the things she feared most was wandering around looking lost, looking new. The first thing that struck her about the school was that the walls were covered with pictures- old houses, photographs of the local landscapes, paintings, poems. It was like walking through a well-kept bedroom. The lockers were beige instead of worn-out military green like Dyersville, and the ceilings were vaulted and contained skylights. It did not feel like school as she knew it, which was a great start. Arriving quickly at the counselor's office, she thanked and was formally introduced to Charles. *"I didn't get your name, ma'am..."* She felt especially rude considering his hospitality. *"OH! I'm so sorry... I'm Sarah Bidding. I'm just so nervous, I forgot."* She smiled her coy smile, and he replied with his own. *"If you need anything Sarah, don't hesitate to ask. You're going to do well here, I can already tell."* He marched back to his post and she entered the office.

Mr. Travers couldn't have been more than 30 years old. He greeted Sarah warmly, and they set about planning her class schedule right away so as not to waste any time getting her started. The class list was shocking- there were literally 10 different writing classes to choose from as well as classes covering what seemed to be every imaginable style and era of literature. Choosing just six was a challenge, but once they had settled, she was pleased and eager to get going. She had taken World History on the recommendation of Mr. Travers and his rave reviews of the professor. Aside from that, she was allowed to hand select her curriculum, and she left the office looking forward to each and every class she had chosen. There were recommended health, personal finance, and physical education workshops every month, but the subjects were not required for daily study.

Mr. Travers took the photo for her school ID, escorted her to her locker and provided a small map of the school grounds, and then bid her farewell. She was on her own, and her first class began in 15 minutes. In five minutes the bell would ring and students would come pouring into the halls. She was fascinated and anxious to see what they looked like, and was also excited to see Angela. Maria had undoubtedly told her that Sarah would be attending Open Door but they had not yet talked about it face to face. Sarah made way towards her first class, and once she was sure of the location, she stood some yards back in order to get a view of the students in the class prior. She pictured ultra-stylish, perhaps snotty, and highly intelligent sorts that would likely not be bothered with her and her commonness. She did not want to appear a simpleton, and hoped that there were at least enough *"normal"* students that she might blend in. She was caught in mid-daydream by the quick ring of the class bell and the reactive shuffle of the students.

There were some that looked exceedingly interesting- deep and pensive- and others that looked like they may have been just an average, run of the mill student at Dyersville. The overall demeanor was much lighter, and five or six students- both boys and girls- said hello to her immediately upon making eye contact. Sarah made sure to have a smile on her face, and took care to not look off-putting or pensive, as she knew she often did when she had a lot on her mind. It was subconscious, but she knew that she tended to look agitated and kept a slight scowl on her face when she wasn't concentrating on doing otherwise. Her awareness of it was something she was counting on to help her exist in peace and harmony at Open Door.

The between-class hustle was a relief in a way... it was no different from Dyersville, and it gave her a feeling of familiarity that she was very grateful for at such a foreign juncture. Her first class was World History, and she waited until a few students had gone inside to make her entrance. The teacher was a 30-something man, good looking, and he caught her eye immediately. *"Hello! I'm Mr. Perry- you must be Sarah Bidding. Welcome."* Sarah was relieved that she didn't have to explain who, what, when, where, and why she was in his classroom. *"Mr. Travers told me you were coming and that you transferred here voluntarily from Dyersville."* Sarah said yes, and smiled, waiting for what seemed to be a punchline. *"Good choice!"* Mr. Perry smiled back, and shook her hand. *"If you don't mind, I'm just going to introduce you to the class briefly. I don't want to make you uncomfortable, or any more so than you probably are already, but I don't want a stranger sitting among them either, OK?"* Sarah agreed, and thanked him, taking a seat against the wall in the 3rd row. Several more students filed in before the bell rang, and Sarah was shocked to see that the small number of desks seemed to be accurate- there were no more than 15 students in the class. The bell rang again, and Mr. Perry took center stage. No sooner had that happened than Angela burst through the door and grabbed the only empty seat. *"Good morning Angela!"* Mr. Perry said, without the slightest hint of agitation in his voice. She looked preoccupied, and had not noticed Sarah. *"Class, we have a new student- her name is Sarah Bidding, and she has just joined us from Dyersville. Apparently she is quite a writer, and seems like a lovely young lady. Please welcome her in your own way."* Most of the class looked over and smiled, minus a few downtrodden-looking boys that stared at their shoes. As soon as Angela heard the announcement her eyes perked up and she found Sarah, greeting her with a smile as only she could. They waved, and gestured to meet after class. In the meantime, and with all possible subtly, Sarah was trying to observe the students in class. With a general demeanor so much different than Dyersville, her curiosity as to what made these students tick so differently was nearly impossible to contain.

The class was interesting, and Mr. Travers had been right about Mr. Perry being a compelling teacher. As soon as the bell rang, she and Angela met in the hall. *"I can't believe you're in my history class!"* Angela blurted out in a tone as excited as she possessed. *"It's a great class, and I'm so happy to see you. Maria mentioned that you were transferring here, but I didn't know when, or what you'd be taking. If you'd like to meet for lunch, I would."* Sarah was already looking forward to the time with Angela. *"I'm glad I'm in your class. It will be nice to see you each morning. I'd love to meet for lunch… When? It says lunch on my schedule as either 4th or 5th period."* Angela's eyes expressed gratefulness for Sarah's kind words. *"I have 5th and 6th, so let's meet during 5th period. 4th period will give you time to wander around and get familiar with things. Most people here are really nice, and the ones that aren't won't bother someone like you."* Sarah was confused by the final statement, but grateful for the idea behind it. She desired nothing more than to exist in serenity at Open Door.

Seeing Angela for lunch would give her something to focus on if her nerves began getting the best of her. She hustled to her next class and remained optimistic and excited for each new moment of the day. Classes had gone very well, and Sarah took none of it for granted, yet by the time lunch and free period rolled around she was tired of being introduced and looked at. After dropping her new books off at her locker she brought just a backpack and the school map on her 4th period journey. She walked the school from end to end, top to bottom. It was truly a welcoming, attractive environment. There were many students that looked foreign, or at least dressed as such, though there would be no way to tell for sure without talking to them. There were students sitting in the halls reading and some were even listening to music through headphones. Her final destination was the library, and she had finally come upon it. There was a prim and attractive woman standing at the check-out desk, and she greeted Sarah upon entering. *"Hello. I don't believe I've seen you before. I'm Stacey."* Shocked that she had been introduced on a first-name basis to what appeared to be the librarian, she approached the desk and returned the favor. *"I'm Sarah- it's my first day today. I came from Dyersville High."* *"Oh! I heard we were getting a couple of you!"* Stacey joked, and then shifted. *"The tragedy there a few months ago really shook this place up as well. We have some very sensitive students, and most of the students here are friends, so the idea of someone meeting their end like that on school grounds was very hard."* Sarah was cautious about how much information to give out. *"It was very hard. The mood of the school wasn't even back to normal when I left last week. It was very troubling."* Stacey perked back up, and apologized. *"I'm sorry- you've been dealing with that first hand for the past month. I'm sorry to have brought it up right when we met. Please enjoy yourself in here, and let me know if you need any help finding anything."* Sarah thanked her, and did her best to get Andrew Mahoney out of her head just as quickly as he had been put back in.

The library was quite impressive. It was bright and spacious, and had a full periodicals section similar to her library in the village. The fiction section was immense, as was the reference section, and she was also quite taken with the quantity of *"alternative"* literature. There was everything from books on bands and music, to Eastern religions, witchcraft, and even books on various cults, criminal organizations, and serial killers. It was more like a bookstore than a high school library, and she couldn't wait to spend more time there. She bid farewell to Stacey, who was probably in her late 30's but looked and acted much younger. She would walk briefly and then meet Angela, and that would be the benchmark signaling that her first day was almost over.

Sarah was headed towards the only remaining section of the school not yet visited when she saw from the back a boy in black jeans and a black coat with the hood up. He was carrying a shoulder bag and walking quickly probably 15 yards in front of her. He must have come from the library, or at least that direction. She began walking as fast as she could to catch up, and had gotten within 10 yards when he suddenly stopped, paused, and turned to face her. She was shocked, and stopped in her own tracks as well, nearly dropping her bag. He did not utter a word, but intently looked her in the eyes; it felt as if he had peered through all her defenses in a matter of just five seconds. Just as Sarah began to unfreeze, he exited through a side door and began running down the sidewalk towards the front of the building. Sarah's legs were like jelly, her hands were hot, and she had gotten a quick chill followed by a prickly warm feeling on her back. It was him.

III.

Sarah tried in vain to collect herself and then redirected towards the lunch area. She was foggy, and partially felt as if the occurrence may have been in her imagination. She could not help but think that he had known she was there, and had followed her either to or from the library. She still felt a little queasy and her legs would not carry her at any speed even if she told them to. The prospect that he was not only real, but was a student at the school she now attended was an emotional overload on this an already heavy day. She felt herself almost ready to cry, but held back at the risk of it being visible to anyone else. She was now able to put a face to the mystery that had been a constant draw on her attention for months upon months, and a beautiful face it was. He looked solemn, but caring, and not the slightest bit uncertain. He looked into her eyes with such an intent and curious gaze that she herself was left wondering who he was looking at. It was clear now that he indeed knew of her, and that many of the *"coincidences"* she had felt in the previous months may in fact not have been. The feelings she had today were reminiscent of the ones experienced at the mall when the boy had intervened on behalf of the younger one. She would have plenty to tell Angela about should she choose to open that door.

Angela had beaten her to their meeting point and was sitting alone on a soft bench looking through a folder. Sarah sat next to her and smiled. *"Sarah, are you OK? You look a little flushed."* Embarrassed, Sarah responded. *"Oh, I'm fine… just nerves on my first day is all. How are you?"* Angela used her telltale eyes to write the part of the story that words left out. *"I'm OK too… just been feeling a little overwhelmed."* Sarah could tell there was more afoot than that, and she was likely just not mentioning it to avoid stressing Sarah during her first day. *"You know, Angela, we haven't known each other for very long, but if there's anything you ever need, I'm happy to be your friend, and I'll be happy to help you."* Angela's sad eyes lit up a little, and became heavy with emotion. *"Thank you Sarah. I don't have many people I can trust, and I can tell that you are someone I can count on. I appreciate that."* They hugged briefly, still seated, and moved on to the topic of her first day. It was nice to have company on her first day, and it finished as pleasingly as it had started. She was certainly tired of being introduced, and was still feeling the mental and physical effects of her 4th period encounter, but had managed to emerge unscathed from the first day at her new school. Her mother picked her up, and the ride home was as friendly an inquisition as had ever been given. Sarah raved about all of it, as she expected her mother would want, and was grateful to arrive home and get to her room. She immediately lay down on her bed and stared at the stars, more preoccupied with the brief face-to-face interaction than she had been with anything in her life. She wanted to find him, and even if they did not exchange a word, she wanted him to look at her like that again. She wanted to know how he found her, and whether it was an accident or something more. In the midst of all this newness, none of it could hold a candle to the interest she had in the only person in her life that had been more puzzling to her than herself.

She drifted to sleep and did not wake up until almost 8pm. She had missed dinner, but awoke feeling urgently like she wanted to explore. Asking her parents' permission under the guise of needing to visit the library, she borrowed the car and had just over an hour until her driving curfew. She snatched up her backpack and hustled out, eating a banana and some almonds in transition, though food was the last thing on her mind. She took the back roads to the village and parked at the far end by the train tracks. Walking up Main St. towards the library, she weaved in and out of each small, windy sidestreet until she arrived at canal trail near the old boathouse. She paused next to a large electrical box for several minutes and surveyed the area. It was a ghost town. There was minor activity outside the Green Tavern, but aside from that, she was the only thing stirring. She walked to the library, poked lazily through a few magazines, and walked back towards her car. She had willed him to be there- she had sent him a message and she was sure he had heard her. Walking as slowly as she could, one of the citizen patrol carts stopped her and asked where she was off to. *"My car is parked at the donut shop, I'm just walking back there to go home."* The old man was friendly. *"I know the curfew has been much looser, but I always check when I see young folks walking alone this time of night. Hope you don't mind. There was a guy in all black hanging around the top of the steps by the library, and he ran off when I approached, so keep your eyes open."* Sarah went cold. He had been there, and she had missed him. She ran back to the library stairs, then around the back towards the parking lot of the village grocery store, and then ran back towards the canal trail. She felt clammy and urgent as if being chased by something, but it was only her piqued curiosity. He was nowhere to be found, and at the risk of missing driving curfew for the first time in her life, she hustled back to her car and headed home.

After breezing through the small amount of homework she had been given on her first day, the wonderment of her introduction to Open Door left her wide awake. She didn't feel as if she could sleep if she had to, and it was beginning to worry her. All her usual tricks would need to be employed tonight to ensure she entered tomorrow rested and recovered... and looking so as well. She had asked her mother to drop her 15 minutes early so that she might explore her new surroundings, but it was really in order to hunt for her boy. The rest of the week had been laid out for her the moment they had set eyes on one another; classes, new friends- they were all incidental and paled in comparison to this new priority. The urgent feelings and rush of emotions was also activating other topics in Sarah's mind. She had some unfinished business back at Dyersville High, and she needed to start planning for it. Carlson and Heffernan were both just as guilty of harming her as Andrew Mahoney ever was, and she had not forgotten. The rejuvenation felt in just the short time she had been away from Dyersville had brought her dark motivations back to light, and had once again set her wheels turning towards revenge.

IV.

With two years under his belt at the Open Door Academy there wasn't much that slipped by Simon's watchful eye. Even though he was not at school all day every day he made his presence quietly known, and used his free time to its' fullest, exploring every alcove and hallway each time as if they were brand-new. He wasn't nosy, just thorough, and felt both a need and desire to keep his surroundings safe and manageable. His grades continued to be outstanding, and his nighttime exploits continued to keep his mind sharp and his senses in tune. The only distraction in his life had just crept up on him and landed at his feet- Sarah Bidding, Dyersville High School junior, had just transferred to Open Door. Simon had spoken with Charles on the morning of her arrival, and was shocked at the development. Sarah was someone that Simon had run across enough times where it could certainly no longer be considered a coincidence, and his interest in her was anything but fleeting. He asked Charles several times if he was sure that was the new girl's name, and eventually believed him after he provided a detailed physical description. Simon was puzzled and intrigued, and had a laugh to himself about both his luck and how surprised Sarah was going to be to see him if, as he thought, she was as aware of him as he was of her. He was caught up on all assignments, and aside from two classes in the afternoon, was not mandated to be anywhere all day. He would find her, and make his presence known.

Grateful for this welcome distraction from the norm, he didn't want to spoil the novelty of their meeting by having it happen randomly. He needed to find out which periods she had free, as he was positive she would be exploring during them. Once again calling on Charles, the only additional information he could provide is that he knew she had been in classes for the first three periods of the day, which very likely meant she had either 4th or 5th period free. The library at Open Door was exceptional, and based on what he knew of her already, he was sure she would make that an early stop. If he were to be *"studying"* in the back corner, he could see her enter and be aware when she left. He positioned himself at the furthest table from the door and waited. He had books with him, as well as his journal, so he was convincing at looking busy. It only took about half of 4th period for Simon's prediction to come true. Sarah meekly entered the library and spent several minutes talking with the librarian. The two exchanged several smiles, and he was again reminded what had drawn him to her so strongly. Her sincerity resonated in every move she made, and when she smiled it was with such feeling that it seemed she may have left a little piece of herself with everyone that witnessed it. She began to explore the library and Simon knew in order to avoid detection he had to get out and wait in the hall. He was able to pack up and sneak out while she was looking at magazines, and he waited around the corner near the restrooms for her to exit. If she turned his way he would begin walking as soon as he saw her leave, and if she turned the other he would follow. He was nervous for the first time in recent memory, and it felt good.

Not five minutes later he saw her pass the checkout desk and he began to walk. He had panicked, and if she turned the other way, his plan would be foiled. He couldn't turn to look now, it was too late. He walked slowly for 10 or 15 yards, heard footsteps behind him in the empty hallway, and sped up. He had lost his nerve, and now he wanted out. The footsteps behind him had quickened and he knew that she had seen him. In a moment of panic, he stopped dead, turned 180 degrees, and met Sarah eye to eye. He had maintained enough composure to engineer his facial expression, and as soon as his eyes met hers, he couldn't have looked anything *but* enthralled. She looked like she may have seen a ghost, and the less than 10 seconds they had spent together had been so intense that Simon lost all nerve to speak, and literally ran for the door. He ran like the devil himself was giving chase, and did so with a smile on his face and cold sweat running down his back.

Everything had changed in the blink of an eye. They had *"met"*, and were now aware of each other in a more formal way. He knew where she would be on a daily basis, and vice-versa. It filled Simon with a fiery courage that made him feel invincible and made him want to explore, and run, and do more things that scared him so that he could again evoke those feelings. More than anything, he wanted to at long last make his return to Wolcott-North and right the wrongs that had been done to him there. The timing was right- the Winter Formal was approaching, so said their website, and he had missed it last year due to what he perceived was not enough time to prepare. The same mistake would not be made here. He had attended the Winter Formal once while at Wolcott and was sure it had remained much the same. If it had, it will be a near-perfect setting for him to gain access to his attackers.

Planning was nothing short of militaristic. He had begun taking notes on the surroundings, and had been visiting in the middle of the night once a week for the past two months in order to familiarize himself. He knew where they would park, where they would be dancing, and most importantly, where they would sneak off to drink, smoke, or whatever else they were going to try to slide past the watchful eyes of the staff. He knew where he would perch with binoculars, and where he would hide close to the building once the time arose. He had his equipment itemized and had done dry runs of packing and unpacking it on the fly. The two things he had not determined were whether he intended to maim or kill his prey, and how he would disguise himself to completely avoid recognition. It would need to appear a random act of violence- robbery would not be convincing as a motive in the woods adjoining a private school- and as he would be a suspect almost immediately once the identities of the boys were released, no detail of disguise could be overlooked. It had to appear to be a maladjusted adult, and Simon had gone as far as securing a voice manipulation device to wear inside a mask. His father had sent him night vision goggles for a birthday several years ago by request, and they would be the missing link in the completion of his project. He had been routinely visualizing it, and it now appeared so real that his hands went clammy and his breath shortened. It felt like reality now, and that signaled to him that his preparation had been thorough, and that it was time. The Winter Formal was two weeks away, and he will have put the final touches on his plan by weeks-end.

The wounds that had physically healed from his beating at Wolcott-North still had power over him emotionally, and he was more than ready to avenge them. Even stronger than the motivation of vengeance was just the pure balance of right and wrong. What happened to him was wrong, and no one had ever made that fact known to the boys. Lisi? Simon was sure to this day that Lisi supported and even helped cover up his beating. Lisi would get his, but not yet. He would wait until he could take something from him that he valued even more than his physical safety. For the boys- the good looking, athletic, popular, cocky boys- he knew what he would take from them. If he chose to leave them alive he will have broken their spirits, taken their confidence, and given them the lifelong scars that fear of the unknown will leave. He will be the thing they have nightmares about and check under the bed for from then on.

Simon was more than halfway home before he even realized he had been running since he left school. He needed to return for two classes in the afternoon, but his mind had been so caught up in the other goings-on that he had all but forgotten his very name. He decided to have lunch at home and then run back. It was still cool outside, and the weather was perfect for clearing his head and getting some thinking done at the same time. Arriving back at school just minutes before his class, he scanned the halls quickly and then entered the science lab. Science was of interest to him for many reasons, not the least of which was the desire to know all he could about chemicals and their properties so that when he chose to do his own research, he had some direction. At one point he had intended to blow up the Wolcott boys cars using some homemade explosives but had deemed it too overt, and even as thorough as he could possibly be, too easy to trace. He was anxious to put to use the things he had learned about chemicals, the human body and its systems, dissection, and even cleanliness and safety in handling toxics… He was ready for graduation to applied sciences. In the context that Simon received it, science seemed almost too dangerous a class to allow a young person to take.

He would certainly see Sarah in the hallways now that they would be looking for one another. The next meetings would not be able to be orchestrated, and he needed to determine in advance if he were going to speak with her, or keep quiet and exit the situation as quickly as possible. He was leaning towards the latter, leaving the inaugural conversation for a time outside school, but he also did not want to be rude or off-putting in a negative way. Never had a social situation created pressure on him in the way that this had. It was truly unique for him in many ways, and whether it happened at school or somewhere else, the prospect of talking to Sarah was almost too exciting to bear.

It was the time of the week for his late-night visit to the Wolcott school grounds. Tonight's goal was timing his approach and exit as he had seen in several books dedicated to military strategy and invasion. He had taken the bus as far as it made sense and then run the rest of the way. Taking the bus on the night of execution would leave him traceable through the on-board security camera, and therefore was not a luxury he would have. Tonight he had brought a black neoprene mask and fitted it with his voice altering device. After exiting the bus he walked a ways, crept behind a shed in a secluded yard, and applied his concealment by flashlight- mask and voice box, gloves, and lastly his goggles. The battery would last over three hours, so even in the event of something going drastically wrong, he would still have quite a bit of time to navigate through the woods with his path lit before him. He had fashioned a custom fitting for the goggles that he hoped would allow him to move at full speed without them bouncing around, and this would be the test run. He switched them on, tightened the waist strap on his backpack, and began to run down the maintenance road at the far end of the Wolcott campus. An occasional car headlight was the only movement he saw, and for that he was glad. He was likely almost invisible, however in the right light there may be a reflection off the lenses of his goggles. They stayed true, not moving an inch even as Simon darted through the low brush on and off the uneven service road.

Upon approaching the school grounds he saw several people in the woods probably 30 yards from where he then stood. It was just too far to make identification, so he crept closer until he was within earshot. Several backs were to him, and those facing him were students he did not know. They were smoking, presumably weed, and laughing. One of the voices sounded familiar, but he could not place it. It was his goal to get as close as he could to the group without being heard or seen. He was within 15 yards when one of the students turned his way but did not see him. The goggles worked perfectly- he could see everything clear as day; it was as if he were invisible and watching unwitting subjects from above. Crawling along the ground, he was careful to conceal his breathing once he closed in on the 10 yard mark. Getting much closer was risky, but based on the thirst for fear that his recent encounter with Sarah had sparked, closer he crept. He was close enough now that he could have spit on anyone in the group- it was three boys and three girls, one of whom Simon now recognized as the nameless boy that had been with David when they shoved him in the hallway prior to his departure. His blood boiled; he longed to attack the group and injure several students in order to make it look random, but resisted, keeping in mind that he wanted David as well as the other boys and would lose his chance if he acted now. Seeing the boy again after all this time brought back feelings in quite a profound way, and Simon now had the motivation he needed to fuel him through the rest of his mission. Scarring the boy that had insulted, shoved, and then later struck and injured him while he was unable to defend himself would be rewarding enough to warrant any level of work, planning, or patience. The time was coming, and his successful visit tonight had helped him swap anxiety with excitement.

Simon was out much later than he had hoped, as he chose to wait until the group left to retreat through the woods. Hearing their inane babble and egotistical, self-centered musings was sickening, and he couldn't get it off his mind on the walk home. He had packed all his gear in the false bottom of his backpack in case he were stopped for curfew violation, although this far out of town it was very unlikely. His pace was brisk, and he was prepared to dart into the dark with the approach of any car. Finally arriving home well after 3am, he ate a bit and went to sleep, resolute and focused on his plan for the following weekend.

Days felt like minutes as the week passed. Simon had seen Sarah several times- they made eye contact, but both had resisted the urge to speak to one another. Possibly she had the same idea about waiting for the right moment outside school to have their first verbal interaction? Regardless, her very presence made every day lively and intriguing, and Simon was sure it had played a large role in the week speeding by. Arriving home from school on Thursday, it was inventory time. Simon went up and down his checklist half a dozen times to make sure everything was accounted for, and then did a final check of his weapons. He was carrying between his person and his backpack an expandable police baton, brass knuckles, a blackjack, a boot knife, a folding knife in his front pocket, a short fixed blade knife in his waistband, and a Taser. He had to be ready for any situation, and also for any decision he chose to make regarding the fate of his attackers. He had layered properly so there was no chance of being affected by the prolonged exposure to weather, and packed snacks in order to keep his energy high should he have miscalculated anything time-wise.

The dance was scheduled to start at 7pm. Daylight savings time had just hit, and as soon as the sun set *(right around 6:40pm)*, he began his journey. He wore a sweatshirt and hat that he planned on discarding once close to the school. His parents had mailed them to him as Christmas presents several years ago and they were neither a color nor a fit that appealed to him. He had only touched them with gloved hands, ensuring they would be untraceable in whatever trash bin they ended up in.

The walk was sobering, and Simon was having difficulty keeping the casual pace that he felt necessary. He wanted to sprint, set up behind the shed he had used before, and wait. His patience returned when he started refocusing on his breathing and remembering the voice of his attacker from the week before. He arrived behind the shed soon after, replicated all the pieces of the puzzle he had prototyped on previous trips, and began the 2nd phase of his plan. He followed the same maintenance road but did not risk using his goggles until reaching his hiding place in the woods. It was now 8:15pm, and he expected to see strays from the herd arriving in the woods shortly. He was close enough to the school that he could hear the music being played in the gymnasium. *"Don't you... forget about me..."* the singer crooned, and Simon found a moment of dark humor, as visions of his two year in the making revenge came clear. It wasn't a moment later that a noise in the woods spooked him and caused him to drop flat to his stomach to avoid detection. Goggles switched on, he began to crawl towards his destination. A dog had spotted him, and was scurrying around looking playful. His first thought was that he had to kill it, but quickly determined that he was not capable of hurting an animal. He lay very still, closed his eyes, hid his hands, and waited. The dog crept close enough that Simon could hear its breathing, and it had even laid down and taken a rest. Eventually losing interest in a dormant playmate, the dog finally got up and trotted off in a direction opposite the school. Simon's heart was racing, as any unexpected situation would have caused on such a tense night. He began to move closer to a small clearing the students called *"the patch"*- an area that administrators were either not aware of or chose to ignore. It was concealed by several large pine trees and was virtually invisible from anywhere outside it. Seated at the top of a small incline, the feature that made it a perfect sneak-away place for students was that you could see anyone approaching from the direction of the school before they saw you. From the direction that Simon would approach, however, you couldn't see five feet in front of you into the dark woods. Simon was 30 yards from the clearing, and had nestled into his designated waiting area. There was no sign of any students yet, and this left him time to snack and rest.

He ate three pieces of jerky, a handful of almonds, and a banana. He took the peel with him, ate while gloved, and used his free hand to lift and return his mask. This deep into enemy territory was no time to be careless. Just minutes after he finished his snack, three girls approached the clearing, one of them carrying a bag and the other carrying a large woven blanket. They spoke quietly, set up their makeshift campsite, and began to laugh nervously as they withdrew a 12-pack of canned beer from a brown paper bag. They began to drink, and talked amongst themselves in whispers that were just too faint for Simon to hear. He watched the girls and thought hard about what they saw in the foolish boys that would join them shortly. He did not think highly of himself, but was by the same token aware that he was much more civilized than the brood that was likely approaching.

The girls seemed to be waiting for something, and before long, it came. A group of four boys quickly made their way up the incline, greeted the girls, and immediately commandeered the beers and began acting boorish. Simon had used the commotion as an opportunity to move closer, and was now a mere 15-20 yards from the students. Simon was met with three of the boys' backs, and the one facing him was of no interest. He did not recognize any of the other boys as David, however the nameless boy that had shoved him in the hallway was present. He was also wearing a hood, which would prove handy during the attack. They all sat in a circle, passing around a joint, and laughing quietly. Knowing they were in no hurry to return to the dance, Simon would wait and see if David arrived. His cutoff was 10pm, giving him about an hour before the battery on his goggles expired, and more than enough time to get out of the woods the long way. He could now hear most of the conversations, and they were again unimpressive and mostly disgusting. It made Simon long to talk to Sarah, and his mind wandered for a few moments until there was a loud bang from the clearing. He looked over and saw a bit of smoke, and several of the girls looked quite startled. The boys were laughing quietly, and not a minute later David and the other boy from the night of his attack came into view. They had thrown a firecracker up the hill, and had thrown another one as soon as they were in sight. The brazenness of the act made Simon angry, and again confirmed his suspicions that several of the boys were, for whatever reason, beyond reproach. Anyone truly concerned about their detection or the resulting disciplinary action would never take such a silly chance.

The time was upon him. The three boys he had waited so long to meet again were just outside arms reach and completely unaware of his presence. He would breathe and focus for five minutes, and then attack.

V.

His sights were set on the three boys- first and foremost David. He held the small fixed blade knife in his right hand, the blackjack in his left, and secured the Taser in his belt. His backpack was strapped tight, his pulse was racing, and his heart was beating loudly and high in his chest.

He went.

Blazing into the clearing at a full sprint, it took a moment for the students to even realize what was happening. Simon kicked David square in the face with the heel of his shoe and followed it with a thrust of the blade to his thigh. David screamed and Simon turned to the nameless boy, who had gotten halfway to his feet and was immediately struck in the head with the blackjack. He staggered, and during the wobble received the same knife wound as his cohort. They were both screaming, two of the girls were clutching each other, and one had already started running down the incline. The third boy had come at Simon and was met with a strong thrust of the blade to the abdomen. The boy hit the ground with a muffled gurgle, and Simon refocused his attention to David. Simon kicked him in the back of the head as he tried to crawl away with his stabbed leg dragging behind. Seated on his back, Simon began ranting almost unintelligibly about privilege, *"you spoiled brats"*, ungrateful youth, all the while striking David about the head and side of the face with the blackjack and his elbows. At this point the other girls had taken flight, and as Simon had expected, so had the other two boys. The nameless boy was writhing on the ground as Simon darted towards him, then Tasing him vigorously in the stomach for almost 10 seconds. His breathing sounded like a purring cat, and he was trying in vain to crawl away from his masked attacker. Simon stabbed his other leg, hit him several times in the face, and let him alone. The third boy was wounded the worst, and Simon knew he was in the most danger of bleeding out. He poured one of the beers on the wound and then forced the boys hand to hold it. He hit the boy in the head twice with the blackjack, told him *"his kind never got what they deserved"* and moved away. The boys were a mess, he heard screams coming from the field below the clearing, and knew it was time to go. He visited David one more time, putting a deep gash across his entire cheek with the small, razor sharp knife. He shouted *"fucking faggots!"* as yet another decoy, and then swiftly disappeared into the woods.

Running as if possessed, he moved at a speed only reached once or twice in his life. He had left the school campus and entered the neighborhood where he would disrobe behind the now-familiar shed. He heard sirens approaching, and knew that if he made it through the next hour he would be both lucky and free. He took off his goggles, mask, gloves, and put on a brown sweater and blue knit cap that he had packed as his return outfit. He took a water bottle out of his bag, wiped his brow with a handkerchief, and began to walk casually through the neighborhoods until he reached the sidewalks to the village and he could run again. He was as nervous as he had ever been, but also felt spectacular. His body and mind were filled with electricity, and he was sure it was bound to burst from within him at any moment. The relief he felt, even though he was still in a great amount of danger, was immense. His plan had gone exactly as he had engineered it, leaving the boys ruined, and the witnesses frightened and bewildered.

The corner of the neighborhood and Thompson Road was where it felt safe to begin running again at full speed, and Simon was ready to do so for the entire two miles until he reached his doorstep. Running with traffic, he saw a police car coming towards him with lights and sirens blaring. He darted behind a large tree and hoped that even though his camouflage was gone he would go unnoticed. The car didn't even slow down, and Simon just as quickly returned to his run. Several cars passed him but he didn't care. He was indistinguishable in the clothing he was wearing, and was moving fast enough that unless someone stopped him, his identity would be safe.

He had made it. Winded, exhausted, and happier than he could remember being since he was a child living with his then-loving parents, he locked the door behind him and set about the destruction of any evidence of his involvement in the attack. He would burn the clothing in the fireplace, along with the weapons, and immediately threw the backpack in the washing machine along with a handful of white shirts and a full cup of bleach. He hid the Taser in the ceiling of the basement and was sad to melt the knife and blackjack, but they could easily be replaced. Keeping a souvenir was a foolish and risky pleasure that he would not succumb to. He had disposed of everything, eaten a hearty meal, and it was finally time for bed. It was nearing 2am, but Simon surely felt it was much later, and slept as soon as his head hit the pillow. He had an unusual dream of a giant spiral staircase, the boys from his attack piled at the bottom, and all the things he desired and loved within reach during his climb into the endless sky.

CHAPTER XII.

Following the aftermath of the attack was as elementary as finding the sun in the sky. News of it was everywhere, and had set the small town into a minor state of panic. It was obvious there were not yet any suspects, and the profiles they were building in the media bordered on nonsensical. Simon thought back to a time just over a year ago when a Dyersville alum was killed and the police came under scrutiny for their poor profiling of the attacker. Although that was a full-fledged murder, the victim was not as prominent in the community or as wealthy as the Wolcott students *(or their parents)* and therefore received much less attention and fanfare. Several of the students present at the attack had been interviewed by local news stations, telling a tale of a hulking man emerging from the woods shouting like a madman and stabbing everyone within range. None of the injured students had spoken out, presumably because they were cooperating with police orders not to. The once-secret spot atop the small hill was no longer, as every news station within a 50-mile radius had used it as a reporting site within hours of the news breaking. Simon sat quietly and watched it all happen, and looked forward to school on Monday in order to gauge the reaction there.

The clue that law enforcement was using as their main lead was a footprint left in some damp earth that could not be identified as any of the students. It was from a size 10 running shoe, which was just enough information to establish the attacker as definitely male, and not much more. The brand and style Simon selected was among the most popular sold- he had asked the salesman prior to purchasing them and remembered being looked at with disdain for not being up on the trends. Untraceable and comfortable were his only goals when picking the footwear; by now the shoes had burned just like everything else, and their ashes flushed down the toilet.

Simon had been out for a walk, and was surprised to enter the house to the sound of the phone ringing. He stared at it for two or three rings, and by the time he chose to pick up the ringing had stopped. Save the quite rare call from his parents or the odd sales call the home phone never rang. He dialed *69 to return the call, and after several rings a woman's voice picked up and said *"Wolcott-North, how may I help you?"* Simon hung up immediately and with a cold chill. Who was calling him from Wolcott? Why? And most importantly, why *now*? The number must have been the main office- Simon felt it unlikely that the school's general number rang through the pay phones, meaning it was someone in the administration that had called. It was not out of the question that Lisi was calling with suspicions about the attack, but was either interrupted or determined his train of thought was ludicrous. Either way, it made all his tedious precautions seem worthwhile. The timing of the call was too strange not to be related in some way to the other night. The otherwise relaxing day was now filled with questions that Simon had no way to investigate, and it made him uncomfortable. That night, for the first time in months, he struggled to relax and sleep. He was relieved that the weekend was coming to an end, as school was just the distraction he needed right now.

Monday morning came and the school was abuzz with talk of the weekend incident. Some students made a mockery of it, expressing *"spoiled rich kids got theirs"*-type sentiments, and others were sheepishly avoiding the topic as if they were nervous for their own safety. Each and every class saw the issue addressed, and the goal seemed to be familiarizing the students with the facts in order to quell the potential fear and hysteria. He was often impressed with Open Door's handling of tough situations, and this was no exception. Simply ignoring something that hit that close to home *(both age-wise and geographically)* would have led to just the kind of conjecture and panic that the rest of the community was falling victim to. Though opinions were divided on the motive, merit, and possible recurrence of the attacks, at least it was being discussed civilly. Or so it seemed.

One particularly odd student named Brian McPherson was vocal in every class as to the *"community service"* that the *"hero"* performed on Friday night. Quite a strong sentiment, even for Open Door, and it was given a pass until the end of the day when a cousin of one of the injured students shared a class with Brian. Mr. Parks was the sociology teacher, and opened the floor to discussion. *"We all know what happened over the weekend- let's take some time now to analyze what may have motivated this sort of attack, and also the effect it is having and will have on the community from a sociological perspective."* Before his sentence ended, Brian again began his outburst. *"Whoever did that is a hero… if more people stepped up to the plate like that, rich snotty brats may think twice about how they act."* Cameron- the cousin- immediately retorted *"That's my cousin you're talking about. He may be a little wild but he's a good person who did not deserve what happened to him in any way. Lay off."* Brian didn't, and instead challenged the point. *"He must have deserved it- that was no random attack. He attacked a bunch of spoiled assholes that were probably going to commit date rapes that night."* Cameron lost it, charged at Brian, and tackled him to the floor while Brian punched at his head. They tussled for a few moments and then several students and Mr. Parks managed to pull them apart. *"BOYS!"* Parks charged. *"Fighting over mere words is unacceptable, even though what Brian said is very hard to deal with. Both of you are one warning away from an office visit, and this discussion is over."* Brian wasn't done yet. *"I would have done it myself if I had thought of it, and next time it happens I hope you're there."* Cameron made another lunge at him and was restrained. *"Brian, please go to the office. I will call in the reasoning for the visit right now. If you're not there in five minutes you are risking suspension."* Parks paused, and fumed. *"You know this is not how we like to do things."* He was right. There was almost never a fight, and even fewer suspensions. The students at Open Door either really wanted to be there, or really needed to be, and both led to a pattern of good behavior.

Upon hearing of the questionable exploits, Simon felt a pang of guilt for the trickle-down effect he had caused. He had managed to remain uninvolved in the discussions, and had been thinking of what Sarah may have thought or said when presented with the situation. He had considered using the topic to start a conversation with her, but decided against using such volatile fodder for their first interaction.

II.

Sarah found herself caught up in the whirlwind that the attack had created. She was enthralled with all details surrounding it, and was glad when the class topic the following Monday turned to them. She kept quiet, but took in all the information and used it to put pieces together. She was no Dyersville police detective, but knew that the attacks were not nearly as random and maniacal as they were made out to be. As someone with revenge on their mind, she could clearly see that motive in another's actions. There was no way to be sure, but she felt strongly that someone had been wronged at Wolcott-North, and set out to right those wrongs last weekend.

Angela was distraught over the recent events, and was in tears when Sarah came upon her. *"What can I do for you Angela?"* Sarah asked sincerely. *"Oh, nothing... I'm just a little caught up in this and can't figure out why. I just feel for the kids that got attacked so randomly... it must have been so scary."* Sarah could not echo these sentiments, however she feigned sympathy for Angela. Sarah knew the look of fear in the eyes of prey, and knew the rush of the attack from the other side. She was confident should the tables ever be turned that she would have the composure and killer instinct to avoid harm if it was thrust upon her. She thought further about the situation from both perspectives, and how brazen it was to attack a group of healthy, strong, young adults, knowing full well that they would be too shocked to mount any sort of counter-attack. She thought as if she were one of the attacked students, and what she would have done. Although impossible to say having not been there, she truly felt she would have stabbed back, or blindsided the attacker while his focus was elsewhere. No more wasting time going down that road. She was the predator, not the prey, and she intended to keep it that way. Putting oneself in a situation where someone can get the jump on you is both foolish and dangerous, and when simplified, she felt that those attacked were engineers of their own fate.

Sarah could not so much as chew a bite of food without thinking of Simon, and the recent events further deepened her desire to speak with him. Hearing his outlook on the attack would do a great deal to prove or disprove the depth of the still-silent connection they seemed to have. An amateurish or haphazard analysis of the events would surely mean that he was not the dark intellect that his pronounced and almost frightening presence would lead one to believe. While she doubted that as even a possibility, it was still nerve-wracking to think of their first conversation bearing that kind of weight. What she longed for was a time outside of her usual parameters *(school, the mall, etc.)* in which to completely engage in the first moments of their communication. She had begun work on putting that together, and would hopefully bring it to fruition in the coming months. Simon was a worthy and welcome distraction, yet she had kept focus on her own revenge therapy in the form of engineering retribution for Carlson and Heffernan. Now that she had been transferred to Open Door, she could more actively *"look after"* them and not risk being found out or noticed doing so. Out of sight, out of mind was a very valid concept for most, but completely the opposite for Sarah. The longer she spent away from Dyersville High, the more she thought about putting every memory of it behind her, and that meant tying up all the loose ends. She had always just thought of Carlson as a buffoon, a myna bird, merely acting and repeating what he thought someone stationed in his position would do. She disliked him for many reasons, but did not share the same loathing for him that she did for Heffernan. Heffernan had demonstrated a true desire and almost an enjoyment of trying to harm her, and through all of Carlson's faults, he was not nearly as malicious as she. Her revenge was not a one-size-fits-all equation.

Due to the uniqueness of her last name, Heffernan was quite simple to locate. Her home address, family status, and even the model of the car she drove were all easily accessible on the internet at the public library. Step one was to visit her home at a time she was surely not there, and the best time to do so would presumably be during the school day. The address listed online was 3.6 miles from Open Door, and would have been an ambitious walk, but a simple drive. She would ask her parents for use of the car and tell a story of picking up several new friends and venturing out for lunch. They would surely bend over backwards in support and encouragement of any manner of normalcy or attempt at socialization in Sarah's life.

Sarah was adjusting well to Open Door, at least superficially, and her parents seemed both relieved and excited at the prospect of their exceptional daughter being in a more fitting environment. *"Mom, would it be possible for me to take one of your cars one day soon? I would kind of like to give a few people rides to school, and it might be fun to go out for lunch. It doesn't have to be any specific day."* Her mother paused for a moment, as if being presented with a steep mental challenge. Quickly her expression shifted. Smiling, she said *"Well Sarah that would be just fine! I'll speak with your father and we'll figure out what day works best for us to carpool. Are you driving anyone we know?"* Knowing very well that what she had asked was impossible, since they had not met a friend of Sarah's since grade school, Sarah responded politely. *"No, they're newer friends. Maybe you'll meet them soon!"* Her mother looked so proud, even though the development was so simple.

She would await the verdict on the car and in the meantime
continue planning for her visit to Heffernan's home. She was
not entirely sure what to look for when she did arrive. Easy
access routes should she need to enter the house, any area of
the landscape that could conceal her, anything that would
prove incendiary if that's the route she chose to go. She had
even thought about booby trapping the exterior of the home,
but felt it would not be a certain enough fate. If found and not
activated, the trap would ruin any further chance of getting at
Heffernan without enormous risk. More than anything, she
was curious about where her target parked, the volume of light
surrounding the house, and visibility from neighbors. The
severity of the attack was also still in question... Sarah had not
ruled out a face-to-face approach, which of course meant that
the conclusion would need to be fatal. There was something
about Heffernan seeing her clearly before being struck down
that appealed to her. Their brief-yet-profound interactions
were so clearly a pissing contest and a power struggle- it felt
almost fitting that the end of their relationship should be as
well. Her plan for Carlson was much simpler, and required no
interaction at all. While Heffernan's fate still stewed in the pot,
Carlson's would be executed just as it had been planned for
months.

It took only a few days of observation to pin down the ritual
he practiced every morning. Parked in the driveway, he left
through the front door and made his way to school right
around 7:10am. Sarah detoured there for one final look on her
way home from the library, hid some supplies in the nearby
brush, and snuck back out and made the two mile trek to
Carlson's home at 1:30am. Sneaking out was not her favorite
means to an end, as it seemed so amateurish and common for
a girl of her age, but this time it would have to do. She dressed

for the occasion, and had another outfit in her backpack should everything go wrong and she needed to evade. The supplies she dropped in her hiding place consisted of six thin strips of balsa wood with more than a half-dozen square-headed nails sticking through each, one roll of black duct tape, four pre-modified and sharpened garden cultivators, one glass cutter, 1lb bag of table sugar, and one funnel. The lighting required to complete her task would surely be the biggest obstacle at that hour, and she said a silent prayer for its adequacy during the last ¼ mile of her walk.

As she arrived at the hiding place, she was delighted to find that the lights outside Carlson's home were not motion activated, but simply left on overnight. She prepared the phase one supplies and then stashed her backpack in the brush. She had set the priority list based on certainty of the result; she took the nail-filled wood strips and the tape, and without a car in sight made her way to Carlson's front porch. With barely a sound, she positioned the strips underneath the braided welcome mat and affixed them securely with pre-cut pieces of tape. The awareness it would require for Carlson, at that hour and in that assumed frame of mind, to avoid stepping on them with his full weight was something Sarah would bet solidly against him having. The nails would easily pierce his shoe, and with any luck, several of them will squish their way into his feet. As she crept back to her hiding place, her excitement for the morning grew. Another half hour of focus would lead to the partial peace of mind that she had been seeking for what seemed like forever.

Anything done to the car was purely to add insult to near-certain injury. She had read often in books on strategy and warfare about the concept of a redundancy system, and had planned a thorough one into this project. Quickly funneling the sugar into the gas tank, wedging the garden tools firmly and inconspicuously under each tire, and then using the glass cutter to scrape deep, sharp divots out of the underside of both front door handles, Sarah's work was nearly complete. If Carlson did manage to get in the car without holes in his feet and gashes in his hands, the sugar in the gas tank *(and as a final backup, the holes in the tires)* should prove the desired day-ruiners. Sarah crudely carved the word *"shame"* in the driver's side window, did a final check of the ground to ensure she had not left anything behind, and prepared to depart.

If only she could see the slow beginning and rapid descent into chaos that her plan will likely bring, or at least the aftermath. Just as she began her twisting walk home through the neighborhoods, it dawned on her: Maria! If Carlson makes it to school tomorrow he will likely be limping, and hopefully driving something other than his own car. She had been meaning to call Maria anyway, and had no doubt that something as odd as a randomly injured school principal would be a topic of discussion. She would use her imagination until tomorrow evening when again her new friend Maria would be of use to her. Sarah made it to the canal trail, took a deep breath, and began to eat an apple. The feelings inside her right now were of fulfillment, completion, and possibly even pride. Not even the finest work she did for the school paper brought her such a sense of accomplishment. She assumed that feelings such as these must be the driving force behind students' compulsion to play on sports teams, enroll in competitive clubs, or even fistfight. She was grateful that she had found something that satisfied her in that way without having to feign interest in being a part of the sickly herd she once attended school with at Dyersville High.

Arriving home in timely fashion and managing to get back to her room without incident, the post- project sigh of relief and subsequent decompression took over quickly, and Sarah fell asleep contented but anxious. Neither the promise of presents under the tree nor the first day of school had ever elicited the nervous anticipation she now felt and had begun to crave. As a strange secondary feeling, Sarah was looking forward to the opportunity to speak with Maria- both for the status report on Carlson, and to enjoy the role of importance she felt in their conversations. Maria was… good for her… and it was a strange but very appealing notion.

III.

Solidly beaten to the punch, Sarah received a call from Maria not long after school had ended. Maria was struggling but entirely failing at containing her excitement and amusement. *"Sarah, you will not BELIEVE the things that happened today… I had to hold myself back from contacting you as soon as I saw!"* Maria's pitch was so elevated that it sounded like an entirely different person. *"Well tell me! I have never heard you this excited and I can't even begin to guess!"* Sarah *had* begun to guess, and was hoping with all her might that the hilarity that seemed to have ensued had something to do with Carlson's appearance in school today. *"Sarah, I don't even know where to start… FIRST, Mr. Carlson- you know, the Principal- came in today on CRUTCHES, with a brace on one wrist, and a scrape right on his head!"* Sarah was as close to tickled pink as she had ever been, and had to focus on breathing so as not to squeal in delight. *"He looked SOOOO mad… he could barely walk, even with the crutches, and looked absolutely foolish with the scrape and bump on his head!"* Sarah had spent the time during Maria's recap formulating a surprised-sounding question. *"Wow! That sounds beyond weird, and must have been so strange to see! Did he get into a car accident or something?"* Utterly shocked that she had managed to sound anything less than elated when responding to Maria, Sarah now had her fingers crossed again for the answer to her question. *"Well, I am not completely sure... but as soon as I saw him, Thomas and I and a few of the others began investigating. About halfway through the day Thomas and our friend Jonathan overheard a teacher in the library saying that it had something to do with vandalism at his house, and that Carlson was looking into certain members of the student body. I'm not even sure what that means, but it sounds more complicated than a car accident!"* Maria sounded pleased at the detective work, and also to share a story that was obviously interesting and new to Sarah. *"Maria, I can't even believe that you guys managed to get the story! I can't imagine they want that publicized... especially if it really was some type of intentional thing! Someone could get in real trouble! Jeez!"* Maria chirped right up and agreed. *"Yeah! I think the only reason they were comfortable talking about it is that Thomas and Jonathan had their headphones in, but nothing playing. We do that sometimes in order to seem distracted but to be able to listen to what's going on around us."* Sarah was so pleased and impressed with Maria, and told her so. *"I'm so glad you called... I've missed seeing you every day, and I appreciate you thinking of me when something interesting is afoot. It makes me feel good."* *"Well, I think of you often while I'm at school Sarah... I don't meet many people that I can relate to and that give me the time of day. And since YOU were by far the most interesting part of my day at school, it's only fair that I keep you up to speed!"* The girls hung up, both certainly feeling camaraderie, or honor among thieves, or at the very least a little bit of contentment knowing there was someone out there with which to share a piece of their eccentricity. Sarah knew that the story Maria had started was far from over, and without seeming over-eager, needed to make sure she was kept up on all emerging details.

Armed with both fulfillment and more nervous energy than she could channel into any ordinary pastime, Sarah turned her attention to the final unresolved Dyersville chapter: Heffernan. The concept was there- it just needed a little deliberateness and a certain endgame. The wavering she had previously felt towards the need for true finality in the situation was no longer present- if she were to clean this slate and not risk any sort of possible exposure or discovery, Heffernan needed to meet her end.

The two mid-day visits to Heffernan's home had been quick, yet the information gathered had been valuable. Her house was quite small, but boasted a decent-sized yard and a driveway that curved and tucked up around the backyard. It appeared that the door off the driveway was the main entry, and that the front door was simply ornament. One house was clearly visible across the backyard, even through the trees and over a small wooden fence; aside from that, the end of the driveway and presumed entryway were quite secluded. Her plan was beginning to take shape, but until the nighttime visit occurred everything was simply speculation. Thursday was traditionally a night that both her parents stayed in; unless something changed, she would tell a story, borrow the car, and make her final dry-run.

IV.

The frenzy surrounding the attack at Wolcott-North had soon diminished with not much more than a whimper. Even in just the two short weeks since, all but the slightest undertones of public concern, or vigilance, or even discussion had lost their hold. Simon was thankful, yet still watchful, and though he was not even a remote suspect in a legal sense, he could not shake the feeling that the recent call from Wolcott-North was neither coincidence nor error, and he was also sure in every inch of his gut that he knew who had placed it. His internal discussion was two-fold- what was HE to do now, and what would Lisi do next? Neither side of the coin was any less complicated than the other.

If his life *(especially over the past few years)* had taught him anything, it was that preparing for the worst was certainly better than having it catch you cold. He knew Lisi was a strong, well-respected member of both the Wolcott faculty and the surrounding community, and should he decide to make trouble for Simon based on suspicions relating to the Wolcott boys, it could easily turn into a forest that Simon may not find his way out of. He was sure that with Lisi's experience and underhandedness that there were more than enough damning notes in his file to cause plenty of trouble- vague enough, of course, to make it clear that Lisi had more concern than contempt for him, but nonetheless incendiary when coupled with the other facts at hand. Lisi was the lone link between the attack in his bedroom, subsequent transfer, and the attack of the boys some time later. No one else on earth- surely not even any of the victims from that night in the woods- would draw enough lines between the three events to connect them in any real way. Feeling an almost palpable sense of panic, Simon decided that the somewhat casual tabs he kept on Lisi needed to be formalized, and that it needed to happen tonight. If Lisi was willing to risk potential discovery by calling his house on an unsecured phone line, there is absolutely no telling what he would do next- or may even be in the process of doing already.

Moving about unnoticed was an art form in and of itself, and one that Simon had worked very hard to become proficient in.

He knew Lisi's car, he knew the area in which he lived, and he knew that several nights a week he visited a warehouse on the outskirts of town, briefcase in tow, and spent several hours there. There was no visible sign on the building, so at this point it was still a guessing game as to what he was doing there or who he was with. The intention tonight was to identify Lisi's house, and tomorrow night's game was to gather as much information as possible about the warehouse. He would need all his wits and energy for the next two days, and even though quality rest was unlikely with the whirlwind his mind was currently caught in, no further benefit was to be gained by simply pacing around and thinking.

With an unusual amount of detachment and distraction, Simon glided through the short time he was required to be at school and then began packing and strategizing for the visit to Lisi's. He knew well that Lisi left Wolcott-North between 4:45pm and 5:15pm and that his house was a 10-minute drive. Simon had found a slightly wooded spot between two houses at the beginning of Lisi's neighborhood, and his intention was to remain there from 4:50pm until he saw the car approach. With binoculars in hand, the hope was to watch him without needing to follow, wait for the car to park and Lisi to enter the house, and then to approach, gather details, and learn a specific address. The only other option was to hope that he parked outdoors, had his name on a mailbox, or something else very obvious; should none of those things be present, he would have wasted a valuable day. He had always felt that things left to chance must simply not be important enough to plan.

There was a fair amount of activity in the neighborhood, and Simon was unsure from the moment of his arrival whether he would be able to remain unnoticed in his less-than-perfect hiding place. In trying to look as inconspicuous as possible, he had a few decoy items in his bag- some wood, a small carving knife, some rope, a few tennis balls, and a small boomerang. Should anyone really begin to question him, he could certainly chalk his presence up to boyhood mischief and get the hell out of there.

Eyes fixed on the road, he sat and waited. Groups of neighborhood kids ran by, laughing and carrying on in ways that Simon was strangely jealous of. They were running as if they did not have a care in the world, and though anger was what he felt, he was aware that it was not *them* he was angry with. Never had he played in carefree whimsy with a group of friends that were there of their own free will; the mood of their run was as visibly different from his as that of a gleeful, prancing show pony and a focused thoroughbred sprinting for the finish line. Several of the children had glanced over at him, but had not even allowed their eyes to fix. It was almost as if they were looking at just another piece of the docile suburban landscape, and that is exactly what Simon wanted.

Finally the dark brown sedan he knew to be Lisi's had turned into view. He ducked as low as possible, quickly secured his backpack, and fixed his binoculars on the car. It was at least two blocks before Lisi even slowed, and Simon was worried that he would drive out of sight and force him to give chase on foot. Not one second before Simon had intended to bolt in the direction of the car did it turn into a driveway at the far end of the street. Simon focused his binoculars and was able to identify the house and then very clearly see Lisi climb out and walk towards the front door. The mere sight of a man whose callousness and arrogance had put him in such danger and caused him such pain was enough to boil his blood, and it was sheer discipline that kept him from running to the house and turning Lisi inside out right where he stood. He waited, and cooled, and as soon as it began to get dark he walked casually from his plain-sight hiding place towards the house that contained the man who had both put his life at risk and held his fate in his hands. Revenge for one will cover both, but neither would go unpunished.

67 Lincoln Terrace- the address was now locked in his mind. After a brief survey of the house and those surrounding it, Simon decided quickly that his plan would need to manifest elsewhere. A close-proximity neighborhood presumably filled with busybodies and window-lookers was no place to roll the dice. The next-night visit to the warehouse became centerpiece in his mind as he took a deep breath and began the run home.

V.

Maria didn't even get a chance to call Sarah to report the latest on the Carlson incident. Midway through the day, Angela stopped her in the hallway and in her usual sheepish, dread-filled tone, began to explain the latest. *"Sarah, Maria asked me to wait to tell you this, but I am a little worried about her and Thomas, and wanted to say something to you now. You know Mr. Carlson was injured, right? Well, I guess he suspects that a Dyersville High student had something to do with it, and after meeting with a few random troublemakers, he has set his sights on those involved with the corridor music issue... and more specifically, those that spoke out in the paper."* Sarah was begrudgingly impressed... It wasn't a Sherlock Holmes-level deduction, but even the fact that Carlson had thought enough into the situation to develop a theory was more than she expected of him. He must be either really upset, really injured, or both. *"...with the music in the corridor again being banned, and this time with real suspensions being handed out for violations, Carlson seems to feel that the students with the most passion about the topic may have reasons to want to stick it to him... Maria went in for an interview today..."* Still not worried in any way, Sarah asked a simple question in return. *"Angela, has Maria told you that she is in some sort of trouble, or that she herself is being blamed for Carlson's troubles?"* Angela stared at her shoes. *"Well, she asked me not to say anything to you. So please don't mention that I did... Carlson told her that they were going to search her locker, and Thomas' also... and that they have to come back in for another interview early next week."* The pauses in Angela's telling of the story were nearly maddening. *"... but the part that she seemed the most upset about is that... Carlson was asking her a lot of questions about you."*

Her attention now fully captured, Sarah felt quick spikes of shock and worry shoot right through her torso. The assumption had to be that Carlson was asking simply because she was the author of the school paper article, and he obviously remembered how things had unfolded with Heffernan and Mahoney afterwards. As the cheerleader for a failed cause, he may think that she would be upset enough about both the verdict and her post-article treatment that she would resort to drastic measures. Although the water was much deeper than Carlson realized, it felt insulting that he may be even the slightest bit near the real reason *(and culprit)* behind his attack. Sarah tried to seem as neutral as possible as she parted ways with Angela, and thanked her for the information. She assured her that things would be OK with Maria and Thomas, and that she would find her later in the day to see if anything else had unfolded.

She was angry... at Carlson, at Heffernan, and at herself for not having thought out the possible trickle-down effect, however unlikely it was. She needed to move forward with the near-complete plan she had been developing- not only just for peace of mind, but to assure Heffernan didn't get involved in the witch hunt that seemed to be taking place at Dyersville High. Carlson was quite obviously a pawn that Heffernan moved at will, and her playing puppet master in a situation such as this could very well spell trouble for her and her new friend. If Sarah were to be brought any closer to the fire it even had the potential to derail Heffernan's impending reckoning.

CHAPTER XIII.

As much as he loathed every single thing he knew about Lisi and cared to know nothing more, Simon's curiosity was strong regarding the happenings within the warehouse he now stalked. On schedule and briefcase in tow, Lisi arrived and made his way into the unmarked, keycard entry door. Simon had walked the building a handful of times, and opted today to simply wait and not explore any further. Ordinarily about a two-hour visit, Simon spent a short time reading magazines at a nearby convenience store, and then swinging on the swings at a small local park. It was cool but refreshing, and the simplicity and rhythm of swinging helped calm his nerves. Simon headed back to his hiding place near the warehouse and settled in for the watch.

The skies grew dark and the temperature dropped, and not soon after, Lisi emerged from the same unmarked door. Looking left to right but not even glancing in Simon's direction, he fumbled with his keys, climbed in his car, and quickly drove off. The alley was wide enough that hiding in plain sight was quite easy, but narrow enough that he will be able to cover the needed distance very quickly and with little noise. There was very little foot traffic on that end of the alley, and though it was lit as if occupied, Lisi was the only person he had ever seen travel in or out of the door. The plan was a simple one, and as long as no one else emerged from the door in the next half hour as Simon sat watch, the next time Lisi exited, he would be waiting.

The half-hour safety net having been extended to 45 minutes, Simon was now approaching unmanageably cold, and was anxious to move indoors. The only thing that raised an eyebrow in the entire on-and-off three hours he had spent in the vicinity of the alley was a sedan parked one block back, running, with lights off. It was gone by the time Lisi had left, but sat still for the entire first hour he occupied the area. Assuming it must have driven off when he made his way to the convenience store, it was chalked up as a consideration, but did not carry enough weight to be a deterrent.

Finally home and fed, this was one project for which there was very little preparation. No special outfit to construct, and only one tool to ensure ready. Focus on his studies would be hard-earned for the next two days, but will again have his full attention by the end of the week. As much as he needed and enjoyed distractions from learning and the regimentation of much of his life, this particular one had been a liability for far too long, and needed to end.

II.

Simply stating that she first wanted to visit the library and then return a sweater she had bought at the mall during the most recent trip with Maria garnered smiles and immediate approval from both of her parents. The ruse of the sweater simply assured no questions would be asked or considered relating to the bag she needed to carry out. A visit to Heffernan's house in the dark was the beginning of the end, and as important as it was to the completion of the project, it would be equally devastating should she be caught or even spotted. She had an outfit chosen, she had a route mapped. She had several key things to look for in the location, and a few that she was sincerely hoping she would not find. Within the week revenge would be handed down and the potential of meddling in the Carlson situation would be squashed; she was finding misguided relief in the idea that Heffernan leaving the picture was as much a benefit to Maria as it was to her. Never one to need a deeper reason or outside justification for the guilty parties she targeted, Sarah found it strange that the idea of assisting Maria was entering into her mental dialogue. She needed to stay focused on the task at hand and the reasons it was that way… She had been intentionally wronged, and it had the potential to happen again. It was not vigilantism, just simple self-preservation.

The corner of the village that she needed to reach was within reasonable walking distance from several of her regular parking areas, but too far to walk from home without being noticed en route, or being extendedly absent at home. She parked at the library, stopped in briefly and checked out a book *(which required a swipe of her library card and subsequent time-stamp)* and then made way on foot. From a vantage point a few houses down, she could see Heffernan's car parked deep in the driveway, and there were several lights on inside the house. Thankfully, the rear entry door itself was invisible from all angles, and it appeared that the small light shadowing the car was either left on or controlled by a switch- she had been sitting still watching for close to 15 minutes and though the area was motionless, it had not gone off.

A light went on in the upstairs of the house, and she knew this was her chance to move closer with the least amount of risk. Quick looks in the side windows showed nothing interesting- bland décor, neatly kept but not striking, and an absence of a comfortable *"lived in"* look. The back of the house told a slightly different story. The rear entryway was messy, and featured a split set of stairs- one that went left and appeared to go into the kitchen and the other that turned slightly and went into the basement. There was a small landing between them, and even considering the slight angle, the stairs appeared almost a straight shot top-to-bottom. The rear door was old, and the locks had never been modernized. Even though her plan had nothing to do with breaking the door or picking the locks, it was important to note all she could in the event something went awry.

Knowing her time was running short she moved to the very back of the house. A row of untrimmed hedges and a large trash bin sat just a few feet from driveways end and gave a perfect view of the street in front while offering the concealment she desired. Even the few moments crouched behind them heightened her senses and gave her a small taste of the whirlwind of panic and relief that she would feel in just a short time. Still sharp and mean, the long-standing animosity and distaste she had for Heffernan added a strange, almost awkward giddiness to her anticipation of the night to come.

III.

Simon was en route when he began thinking about both the emotional freedom and free time that would be bestowed upon him when this night was over. He thought, as he often did, about the manner in which he wanted to first speak to Sarah; Location, topic, dress... just as with his much bleaker projects, he wanted to leave nothing to chance. Nothing had ever captured his attention and distracted him from himself in the way she had. He was equally as nervous about the build-up as he was about as the meeting itself. What if she was not truly the intriguing, dark, brilliant, muse that he had turned her into in his mind? There was no use in thinking that way, he told himself. If she was, he will have found what may be the most important treasure of his life. If she wasn't, he will be no worse off than he is now, and should be thankful for the much-needed softening of his usual internal dialogue.

Just blocks from the alley, he began to rehearse both movement and verse, and to mentally settle in to what was about to transpire. Simon had decided long ago that he needed to convey one simple message to Lisi, and that he wanted to look him in the eye while doing so. *"I'm surely not the only one you've made feel like an outcast at that terrible school... This is for all of us..."* Simple, yes, but also all-encompassing- and if the entire truth be told, unarguable even by Lisi himself.

The alley itself, the spot in which he was to wait, and even the lighting all seemed just as he had hoped. There were the usual amount of cars- no more, no less, and a chill in the air that had seemed to minimize foot traffic. He crouched down, double-knotted his shoes, pulled his collar up high underneath his hood, and then put his hands in his gloves. Since there was a chance they would need to be destroyed whether things went right or wrong, he had worn his back-up jeans and an older sweatshirt- both the same size, style, and brand as the others, but just lacking the polishedness of an outfit he would wear to school or in public. If the previous observations were accurate indicators, Lisi would make his final exit within 15 minutes. Simon slowly surveyed all there was to see up and down the street one final time… Just as he exhaled a sigh of relief, he saw it: The sedan from his previous visit, no more than two blocks down the street- only identifiable by the trickling of exhaust into the pale black night sky.

Any thought given to the discovery was brought to an abrupt halt when the first floor light that signified an approach to the keycard door had turned on. The die had been cast, the puzzle had been completed- car or no car, he would follow through no matter what. His resoluteness would need a more suitable challenger to back it down.

A mere ten seconds later Lisi emerged, and Simon went.

IV.

The only discomfort Sarah felt towards the situation about to unfold was that of the men's sneakers she was wearing over several pairs of thick socks to avoid leaving any traceable footprints. She had planned for an event of this nature as much as fate would allow, and now that the wait was over, focusing her attention and double-checking her list were the only steps left to take. The walk had felt long- it *was* long- but the impending relief would have fueled nearly any length journey. Sarah took care to fiddle with something in her pockets or tie her shoes to shield her face from view of anyone she met along her walk; it added extra time, but was certainly not a waste of it. She recalled the volume of commotion over Todd's death outside the Green Tavern, and knew that the fuss made over Heffernan would make that look like a single candle on a birthday cake. She was now within sight of the house… Pausing to take a few deep breaths, she felt both prepared and excited to finally pull this curtain closed.

The motive would be robbery- Sarah had taken an envelope from the local credit union where many of the teachers at Dyersville High did their banking and scrawled on it, left-handed, "$500". She had decided to crumple the envelope and leave it at the scene, and after completing her task, take anything of even remote value that Heffernan had in her possession and flee. Possibly the attacker had been watching and followed from the bank? She could not guess the conclusion that would be drawn, and she didn't care. She simply needed to divert suspicion in any direction but hers. She walked crisply but calmly to within two houses of her destination and then sped up, crouched down, and breathed slowly. She was relieved to find Heffernan's car in the exact spot she had hoped, and set about peering cautiously in the windows to assure she was the only one home. Able to catch a glimpse of her target moving around the kitchen, she knew that now was the time. It was dark, but not late, and although she would surely be viewed as a strange visitor, she was more than certain that curiosity would force Heffernan to take the bait. Sarah was hidden behind the hedges for just long enough to secure all her belongings and shift her demeanor. She took her hood down, shook her hair out, unzipped her sweatshirt and approached the door with a docile look on her face.

"Who is it?" Heffernan asked from the kitchen as she was

walking towards the small landing. *"Hi, Ms. Heffernan…"* The pause allowed the teacher to make her way to the door, and she looked as confused as she did surprised at the face that looked in at her. *"Sarah… Bidding? What are you doing here? This is highly unusual."* Sarah manufactured the meekest smile possible and gave her answer. *"Well, I have been feeling really badly about several things that transpired over the past year or so, and my parents have encouraged me to seek out those that were affected by them and attempt to make amends."* She tilted her head down as if to look at her shoes, but kept both eyes on the door. Heffernan looked at her through an extended pause, pulled closed the front of the sweater she was wearing, and finally turned the lock. Indulging her last act of insolence, Sarah waited patiently as she took her sweet time in unlocking and opening the door. As soon as she did so, Sarah burst in and without even the slightest pause, shoved her straight down the steep basement stairs.

The noise she made during her fall was like nothing Sarah had ever heard. The closest thing to it was the moment the car struck the boy at the park, but that was once, and faster. Sounding like a bouncing, wet tennis ball, Heffernan thudded and smacked her way to the bottom… after pulling her hair back and tying her hood up, Sarah hustled down right behind her. She was badly injured and was attempting to speak but could only muster a series of whispered words and head shakes. She pushed with her feet, but the only anchor she could find was a small piece of railing. It succeeded in moving her about a foot, and that was the last offense that Heffernan would ever mount. Sarah had found a few things in the basement that she could use to cause the harm she needed, and opted for a fire extinguisher. Heffernan pawed with her left hand as a last-ditch protest, and as she did so Sarah dragged the extinguisher down from overhead on to her legs. Her scream was muffled, and before striking her once more in the same manner, Sarah looked her in the eye. It was a mistake she was not quite prepared for, and it momentarily shook her focus. Something suddenly began brewing inside her, and before it went any further she needed to finish what she started and get herself to safety. She looked once more at Heffernan and then swung the crude tool down on to her head with all her might. Her hands buzzed, and she couldn't tell if it was from the physical act itself, or something else. She composed herself as best she could, planted the receipt near the purse she found hanging in the rear entryway, took the cash and credit cards out of the wallet, and exited the situation.

The unmistakable facial expression Heffernan had exhibited *(only brought on by the hopeless acceptance of fate)* had spun her back to the unfortunate, unforgettable view she had into a neighbor's home as a young girl. The near-violent confrontations between husband and wife, escalating in severity as each month passed... the icy, malicious glares between them... the pretend kindness and happiness engineered for the benefit of the young children, and the collapse into ruins as soon as they were out of sight. The private unraveling of the young wife followed by the husband's often rough and loveless *"consoling"* of her... all of it shook Sarah's nerves, matured her sensibilities far quicker than sanity would endure, and engrained a mistrust for even those closest to her that she began to feel was necessary for survival. She watched day after day as if it were on television, until she finally witnessed the wife's spirit broken and her hope die. Though not a physical death, even from Sarah's very young perspective, there was no coming back from such a descent.

Soon after *(when Sarah was barely 11)* the woman had

disappeared from view for a period of time. Thinking it appropriate to ask about the neighbor, Sarah inquired one morning over breakfast and was met with an uncustomary, curt response. *"Sarah, Mrs. Andrew left, and will not be returning. Please do not mention anything of it outside our house."* Her curiosity was piqued; she was very young, but astute, and knew that the woman did not simply *"leave"*. Her mind immediately went to murder, but being that the husband and children were still in the house and her mother obviously knew some particulars of the situation, it shifted to suicide. It was a concept she did not quite understand, but had seen articles about in several magazines at the doctor's office. She had once thought it to be something that only happened to youth, but in reflecting on what she had witnessed over the past year, she felt an odd sense of calm in thinking of the woman resting somewhere safely and quietly.

Shivering, Sarah began to truly cry for the first time she could remember… both the unexpected visit to her childhood and the sheer weight of the ordeal from which she was fleeing made her feel as if she may have taken a victim, not simply righted a wrong. With arms aching, she ran as if being chased. Feeling the cold course inside her as if it had replaced her warm blood, she longed for nothing more than the isolation of her second-floor sanctuary in her parents' simple house; as it sat quietly on its clean, basic cul-de-sac, camouflaged by a sea of similar fish, it had not a single hint or clue or heard even a whisper of the dark, twisted *(yet somehow reconciled)* secrets it contained. The house had no choice but to shield and accept Sarah's secrets and abnormalities. As the fury and panic and hurt she now felt grew and overcame her, it became newly clear that she, too, had no choice; There was no way to escape, no way to erase, and no way to reverse.

Her longing for the comfort she had felt in human embrace momentarily softened her pace and made her want to stop running and lay on the ground. Nothing short of the deepest understanding of what had just transpired could have kept her moving forward; the crushing weight of unprecedented emotion she felt was both a hindrance and just alarming enough to keep her in check and on track. The feeling of being chased was one she could not ignore, and turned to look behind her every chance she got. Not 200 feet from the final turn before her home stretch, she again snapped a quick look over her shoulder, tripped, and fell on the last patch of concrete sidewalk before it turned into grass. The physical pain now howled in unison with the rest, and while lying on the ground briefly indulging the moment, Sarah first realized that she may have opened an un-closable door. She had taken a life with her hands, and while previous actions had led to similar results, they had each felt at least a tree branch length from her fingertips.

Her attention needed to be diverted. The cold, hollow ache she was attempting to fight off with common sense and clarity could easily win the battle should she not succeed in putting it back in its proper place amidst the other common human emotions she chose not to indulge. She would not let this be the undoing of her. She needed to see Simon- she needed to feel what he alone made her feel- and it needed to happen soon.

Upon arriving home and taking all the necessary precautions to conceal, dissolve, or destroy any evidence of her that-night whereabouts, she allowed herself time to grieve. She hid in her closet and cried with her head in her hands until she could no longer hold it up, and then buried it in a pillow. She felt as if she were crying for each and every life that had ever been touched by the cold hand of death, and mourning for all the ones that had been so unjustly. Again the memory of the neighbor swept through her thoughts, and she considered for a moment how different things might have been had she not witnessed that year of unyielding pain and abuse. She wondered how she had remained so composed for so long, and why this moment felt as if it were making up for all the lost indulgence of feeling over the years. She was shaking, and more than anything on earth she wanted to tell someone what she had done. She wanted to tell someone what she was feeling... and why... and have them tell her it will all be OK, but she knew that was not a part of the path she had chosen. The path of solitude is one that few can endure, and even fewer can embrace. She was learning that although it is a mode of existence she knew well, it may not be something that she can safely manage for much longer.

The weight was not lifting but the thought of speaking with Simon, and the fantasy of having such conversations with him, began to at least quiet the storm. She had been spending much of her non-library time playing *"process of elimination"* with his whereabouts, and had gathered at least enough useful information to find him outside the confines of Open Door and possibly even speak to him for the first time. It was this type of thing that got people through their pain and suffering, Sarah thought. Even just imagining something appealing to her was helping neutralize the very non-imaginary memories of both distant and recent brutality. She spent a minute thinking of Angela, and realized now why she had always selected fanciful or mystical reading when they visited the mall. Imagination was her coping mechanism... and although she was sure their imaginations played out quite differently, she

221

could at least now see and appreciate the similarities. Sarah took a shallow, exhausted breath and began to plan again; Imagination alone was not enough to guide her through the murk that both her actions and emotions had dragged her into. She had reached what she felt to be a point of no return- her sole focus had become the fact that *her* coping mechanism was flesh and blood. He was the only speck of light on the dark trail; he was the only one that watched over the weak. Her path having gone dark, and her will having gone weak, she needed him now. It was time- and she knew exactly where, and exactly when.

V.

Finally the planets had aligned. They were nearly face to face- no interruptions, no distractions inside the breathing stillness of the night. The alley was dark, and there was a thick east coast fog looming overhead. The situation was almost inconceivable, but after months of planning, Sarah had pinned down all there was to know about Simon and it had led her here. There were cars lining both sides of the alley, and lights on in the buildings surrounding them, however it felt to her as if they were the only two people on earth. She had taken care to look her best, and as always, she was impressed with the somewhat elegant simplicity of Simon's look and the dignity and confidence that radiated from it.

As she was admiring him from just more than ten yards away, a door opened to the right and out walked an older man carrying a briefcase and looking nothing short of terrified the moment his eyes laid on Simon. He put the case down and withdrew his keys from the front pocket of his coat, inching towards his car door. Simon moved quickly towards him and Sarah became momentarily frozen in anticipation. The alley was dead silent, and the next sound she heard was Simon whispering something to the man with a quiet hostility. Before she could even think of what to do next, Simon had drawn a blade from his belt and thrust it into the man's neck. He gasped, clutched his throat, and fell to his knees. Simon drove the blade several more times into his already wilting body, and then proceeded to take his wallet, take the briefcase, break the car window with his elbow, and then *(to her utter and surely visible shock)* he ran to her, seemingly not even considering the brutality of the act he had left in his wake.

"Hello Sarah." He said, as calmly as if they were being introduced for the first time in home room.

She waited, absorbing the moment, and feeling like a young child looking up at a real-life incarnation of a superhero.

"Hi Simon."

ABOUT THE AUTHOR

Greg Walsh has walked upright down a path of resistance for most of his life. The discovery of BMX bike riding and hardcore music in early adolescence derailed the train of convention and sparked a love affair with the underground that continues to burn strong. Channeling the creativity that had been misguidedly relegated to youthful mischief and wrong-righting, Greg immersed himself in counter-culture. Through patience and perseverance, he began to make marks of his own within it, and has never looked back.

Writing intertwined itself with all his successes and setbacks, and has served as chronicle to the strange and often dangerous occurrences that were never far behind. Greg's non-fiction storytelling has been both catharsis and corruptor; if any resolution was found, it has never been without shining harsh light into dark corners, and being made to look.

In fiction, Greg creates characters that we either want to run towards and embrace or run screaming from, appeasing the notion that sometimes what appalls us on one hand, appeals to us in-kind; the strongest responses in his life have been evoked by things in equal part good and evil.

Theft of the Age, Volume 1 is Greg's first full-length work of fiction. He has also published *'War of Attrition'-* a non-fiction anthology filled with stories, letters to real and imaginary people, and unnerving cultural observations.

Driven by discontent, Greg continues to scheme, write, subvert, struggle, and progress, and aims to provoke many others to do the same.

He currently lives and works on the east side of Rochester, New York.

CPSIA information can be obtained
at www.ICGtesting.com
Printed in the USA
LVOW13s2202190217
524731LV00016B/1258/P